The Shadow Garden

The Shadow Garden

Andrew Matthews

USBORNE

First published in 2005 by Usborne Publishing Ltd., Usborne House,
83–85 Saffron Hill, London EC1N 8RT, England. www.usborne.com

A CIP catalogue record for this book is available from the British Library.

JFMAMJJAS ND/05   ISBN 0 7460 6794 1   Printed in Great Britain.

In respectful memory of
M.R. James,
the master

Contents

The Story

In the old days they used to tell stories like this in winter, with night and frost black and white in the windows, and a cold wind moaning in the tops of the chimney pots. This is the sort of story that makes people turn on more lights to chase the shadows from dark corners. It's my story.

It happened a long time ago when I was young and not shrivelled up like an old apple as I am now. The world was different then, slower. There were no televisions or radios; a car was a rare sight and a rattling, clattering sound.

Here's a photograph taken outside the schoolhouse in Little Harding, the village where I was born and brought up. There I am, first on the left in the back row – Matilda Brand. Only no one ever called me "Matilda", I've always been "Matty". If you look closely, you can make out my wide eyes, turned-up nose and mousey hair. I'm not tall or short, not fat or thin, not pretty or plain – ordinary, that's me. The woman on the end there, with a face like she's got something that smells bad stuck to her top lip, is the teacher, Mrs. Ellerby. She wasn't nearly as stern as the photograph makes her seem.

I remember the day it was taken; I remember lots of things. In many ways the past is clearer to me now than the present is, especially on nights when the dreams come.

The dreams are making me tell the story. I hope that once it's told, the dreams will stop.

The Gift

I've always seen things that other people can't see. Ma once told me it was because I was born on a Sunday when decent folk were at church, but I think it's something older than churches, something as old as stone, that looks out at the world through my eyes. Of course, at first I thought I was the same as everybody else. If I ever talked about the things that I'd seen, people would laugh and say it was no more than childish nonsense. But when I was six, I discovered that I was different, and I began to understand what I was seeing.

That summer on a baking hot day, Ma and I were walking through the village. I can't remember where we were going, but I remember the way we went – along Brook Lane, and onto Church Road, past St. Stephen's. It was hot and the air shivered so that the stones in the churchyard wall seemed to be dancing. I heard someone chanting, turned my head to look and saw a small group of people gathered around a freshly dug grave. Reverend Turlip was doing the chanting, and he held an opened prayer book in his hands.

"What are those people doing?" I asked Ma.

"That's poor Sammy Byers's funeral," Ma said in a low voice.

I frowned. "Sammy from down Mill Way?"

Ma nodded. "He took a fever the doctor couldn't do nothing for, and they're burying him today."

A laugh came shooting out of me like sparks flying up from a bonfire.

Ma's eyes went wide and round. "What are you laughing at, Matty, you wicked girl?" she demanded.

It was hard to laugh and talk at the same time. My voice gurgled as I said, "Sammy's playing a trick. He can't be buried because he's not dead!"

There was thunder in Ma's face, and it rolled away my laughter. She caught me by the arm and said, "What d'you mean, he's not dead?"

"He's standing over there," I said, pointing. I could see him plain as plain, standing in the shadow of the big yew tree near the churchyard gate. His straw-coloured hair stuck out all over the place and his face was pale. He wrung his hands together and hopped from foot to foot as if he needed to pee. Then he noticed that I was staring at him, and he stared back. The darkness of his eyes made me shudder and a weariness crept over me, as if my strength was running out through my feet.

"Are you sure it's Sammy?" said Ma.

"Certain sure!" I said.

By now I was frightened. The tightness of Ma's

grip on my arm told me that I was in trouble, though I didn't know what for, and I was so tired I thought I might drop down in a faint.

"Don't you ever tell no one you saw him, hear me?" said Ma, hissing like a cat. "Not ever!" She yanked my arm and dragged me down Church Road.

"What is it, Ma?" I wailed. "Why are you so vexed with me?"

Ma said nothing until we were well clear of St. Stephen's. She marched me to the wooden bench at the edge of the Green, plonked me down and sat beside me. I felt better now that I'd left Sammy behind me, and resting on the bench soon brought my energy back.

"You've got a thing that makes you special, Matty," Ma said, "but you'd best keep it a secret."

"What thing?" I said.

"It's what you did when you saw Sammy in the churchyard," said Ma. "Not many see the way you do, and most people would be scared of you if they knew you could do it."

"Scared of me?" I said. "But I'm only a pennyworth of nothing!"

Ma shook her head. "You see the departed, Matty," she said. "Them as is waiting to cross over to the other side."

"The other side of what?"

"Life and death," Ma said. "When someone dies sudden-like, there's a part of them that doesn't want to leave this life. They walk about where they used to walk, pretending there's nothing wrong."

"Like...ghosts?" I whispered, and saying it sent a shiver through my blood.

"Just like ghosts," said Ma. "You've got the gift of seeing them and you must keep it to yourself – unless you want to be called a witch."

"I'm no witch!" I spluttered.

"Ah, you may know that and I may know it, but others don't," said Ma.

I glanced down at my shadow on the ground and wiggled my fingers to make my shadow wave at me. "Can ghosts hurt me?" I said.

"Do no harm to them, and they'll do no harm to you," said Ma.

I'm sure that Ma really believed this and I believed it too, but in time I discovered that the relationship between the living and the dead wasn't quite so simple.

That wasn't the last I saw of Sammy Byers, not by a long chalk. Night after night I heard him sobbing outside our cottage. If I kneeled up in bed and peeped out of the window, I could see him looking at me with his lost eyes, whimpering and grizzling. At first I felt sorry for him, but as time went on he became a blessed nuisance. He wasn't the Sammy Byers that I'd known, just that part of a person that Ma had told me about, all hungry and lonely and not belonging anywhere. He couldn't hurt me, just like Ma had told me, but he made me tired. It was as if his spirit took strength from me so that he could stay in this world for a bit longer.

But my childish strength wasn't enough, and in the end Sammy wore out. He grew as thin and faint as the head of a king on an old coin, and one night he just wasn't there any more. I guessed that he'd crossed over and I was glad, glad for myself as well as him, because I could sleep in peace again.

So I learned to live with my seeing, and to keep my mouth shut about it. Ma had called it "the gift", but it seemed a funny sort of gift to me, one I hadn't asked for, and one that wouldn't work the way I wanted it to. For there was one ghost I longed to see but couldn't, no matter how hard I tried.

The Conversation

3

I never knew my pa. He caught the cholera from drinking bad water and died, while I was a baby. It doesn't seem fair that you can die from drinking water, does it? But that's what happened to Pa.

I've no real memories of him, just bits of pictures that I imagined from what Ma told me. He was a good man so she reckoned, tall and strong and not afraid of hard work. His name was Matthew Brand – Matty Brand, like me. Pa's grave was in St. Stephen's churchyard. We were too poor to buy a headstone for his grave, but I knew the place where he'd been buried, and I used to visit sometimes on my way home from school. I don't know when or why I started talking to him, but before long it had become a habit to tell him about the wishes and fears that I never told anyone else, for there was nobody else that I could tell. Because my seeing had to be a secret, making friends didn't come easily to me. Somehow the other children sensed that I was curled up on myself, like a woodlouse, and they left me alone. I didn't talk to Ma about my worries because she had enough worries of her own to be going on with.

Pa didn't leave us with much when he died, and Ma had to work hard to make ends meet. She did anything that came to hand – washing, ironing, needlework – but what she did most was skivvying, cleaning houses. There was more than one well-to-do farmer's wife round us who couldn't afford a housemaid but still fancied herself as being above doing housework, so they paid Ma to do it for them. Trouble was, she had to walk a long way in all weathers, and she'd come back home tired out. I wanted to work to bring in more money, but Ma wouldn't let me leave off going to school. She said the pennies we paid to Mrs. Ellerby were well spent.

"Learning is a way for people like us to get on in the world," Ma used to say. "We can't be rich so we have to be clever instead."

Poor Ma! She never had any schooling herself, but she was dead set on my being schooled, which wasn't always easy for me. As I got older, other children began picking on me and calling me names behind my back. They say that being called names can't hurt you, but it can. You hurt deep inside where no one can see.

One afternoon, not long after my fourteenth birthday, I stopped off on my way home from school to talk to Pa. Even when it was at its busiest, Little Harding wasn't what you could call a noisy place, but the churchyard was always extra quiet, like a silence inside a silence. I spoke to Pa about school, about how Ada Heston bullied the other girls and made up

games that left me out, saying that only girls with living fathers were allowed to play them.

Then I told Pa about Ma. "I worry about her," I said. "She slaves away day and night, but there never seems to be enough money, and now the landlord's going to raise our rent. Ma will get sick if she carries on as she's going. I want to help her, but I don't know how. What should I do, Pa?"

First I heard a single whisper, then another and another, and all at once my ears were filled with a noise like a strong wind in the leaves of a weeping willow. Every spirit and every memory in the churchyard wanted to talk to me, and they were all greedy for my strength. If I'd let them, they would have drained me dry and left me as withered as a dead spider.

Someone behind me said, "Who are you talking to, young lady?"

I was that startled, my bones nearly jumped out of my skin. I spun round and saw the whiskery chops of Mr. Riddell, the church sexton. He was sucking on a stubby black pipe that had no tobacco in it.

"No one!" I snapped. "I was talking to myself – not that it's any of your business!"

I was sharp with him because he'd frightened me so.

Mr. Riddell's bristling eyebrows went up. "Ain't you got no respect for your elders?" he said.

"I respect my betters," I said, "and I've been taught that elders and betters aren't always the same thing."

Mr. Riddell took the pipe from his mouth, turned his head, spat and chuckled. The chuckling sounded like a bear snuffling about in his chest. "That's a sharp tongue you've got there, Matty Brand," he said. "Mind you don't slip and cut yourself on it." He smiled a smile that had more gaps than teeth. "I know who you were talking to. I talk to 'em myself sometimes."

My face went numb with shock. I was convinced that Mr. Riddell had guessed my secret and would spread it about until the whole village believed that I was a witch. All I could do was try to bluff my way out.

"Talk to *whom*?" I said, scornful-like, showing off my schooling.

"Why, the dead," replied Mr. Riddell. "I find it very calming. They've got no gossip to spread, no scores to settle and they're quite happy just to listen."

I could have laughed out loud with relief. It was obvious that Mr. Riddell didn't know anything about *really* talking to the dead, or he would have mentioned how bewildering and exhausting it was.

We chatted about not very much for a minute or two, and then I set off home. I gave little thought to my meeting with Mr. Riddell, but it was to prove extremely important to me. Though I didn't know it, he had overheard every word of what I'd said to Pa, and that started off a chain of events that was to change my life for ever.

Glad Tidings

Four weeks after I met Mr. Riddell in the graveyard, Reverend Turlip paid Ma and me a visit. He arrived one evening at six o'clock. Ma, who hadn't been expecting him, flapped about like a hen.

To tell the truth, I didn't much like Reverend Turlip. He was an important person in the village, being the vicar and everything, but he was nowhere near as important as he thought himself. There was something altogether too smug and self-satisfied about him.

The reverend refused Ma's offer of a cup of tea. He hooked his thumbs in the pockets of the waistcoat that was stretched tightly across his plump belly, and his oily black hair gleamed in the lamplight as he said, "I am the bearer of glad tidings, Mrs. Brand."

"Oh?" said Ma. "What tidings might they be?"

Reverend Turlip puffed up his chest the way he did before he started a sermon.

"I know that your circumstances have always been somewhat straitened," he said, meaning that we were poor; Reverend Turlip would never use a single word when half a dozen would do, "and just recently a little bird told me that you are having trouble making ends meet, so I have taken it upon myself to lend you some assistance."

I knew right then and there who the little bird was, and my heart sank. Mr. Riddell must have told Reverend Turlip what I'd said to Pa about Ma working so hard and having nothing to show for it, and the reverend had decided to get on the right side of the Almighty by interfering in our lives.

Ma went from a hen to a terrier with fur standing up on its back and a growl rattling in its throat.

"I don't want no charity!" she said.

Reverend Turlip smiled a pleased-with-himself smile. "My dear Mrs. Brand, you misunderstand me. Allow me to explain. Having been apprised of your predicament, I felt it incumbent upon myself to—"

It's no use! I can't bear to write down his words. The sound of his voice turned the air into lard that stuffed up my nose and mouth until I could hardly breathe. The long and short of it was that Reverend Turlip had been reading a copy of *The Fenland Gazette*, spotted an advertisement for a housemaid and replied to it, recommending Ma for the post.

Ma was proper flummoxed at this news. "A housemaid – whereabouts?" she said.

"At Tagram House. It lies on the coast, just outside Derlingham," said Reverend Turlip.

"But that's more than ten miles away!" Ma gasped. "How would I manage the journey every day?"

Reverend Turlip gestured airily. "The terms of employment include accommodation."

"And what's to become of me while Ma's living in Derlingham?" I piped up.

Reverend Turlip responded to my sharp tone with a slow blink and a frown that showed he didn't care for me any more than I cared for him.

"There's the beauty of it, Matty," he said. "I mentioned you in my letter, and the reply I received offered both you and your mother an enthusiastic welcome. You may join her in the employ of Dr. Hobbes."

"A doctor?" I said. "We'll be all right if we get sick, Ma."

The reverend's laugh came down his nose and made me feel small.

"Dr. Hobbes is not a medical man, Matty," he said. "He is a Doctor of Philosophy and was once a professor at Cambridge University."

I had no idea what philosophy was, but I didn't want Reverend Turlip to see my ignorance, so I shrugged as though I couldn't care less about doctors and universities.

"His man, Mr. Vaughn, is coming here to interview you both at the Walnut Tree Inn on Friday morning," continued Reverend Turlip.

"The best inn in the village," I said, which was meant as a joke, because it was the *only* inn in the village.

Reverend Turlip gave me a look like he didn't see the funny side of it.

"Your appointment will be at ten o'clock," he said. "Pray don't be late."

"Oh no, sir!" said Ma. "Much obliged to you I'm sure, sir."

When Ma and I were on our own again, I said, "Who asked the vicar to stick his beak in?"

"Now, Matty!" scolded Ma. "The reverend only did what he thought was right. We ought to be grateful."

"Huh!" I said, not wishing to be grateful to Reverend Turlip for anything, but there's no denying that I was curious. Although I wasn't that fond of school, what with having no friends, I loved and respected learning, and the idea of living in a grand house with a famous professor excited me. At the same time, I felt anxious about leaving Little Harding and going off into the strange wide world.

"The fact is that we can't afford to stay in this cottage much longer, Matty," said Ma. "We won't be any worse off in Derlingham than we are here, and at least we'll be together."

Ma was right, there was comfort in the thought of our togetherness. I put the thought by for a time when I might need it.

At the Walnut Tree

That Friday Ma and I dressed in our Sunday best. Ma was nervous. She fussed over her hair and chided me for every little thing before chivvying me out of the house, through the village and into the Walnut Tree, where we asked for Mr. Vaughn. The pot boy took us upstairs to the private room, knocked on the door and called out, "Your visitors have arrived, sir!"

Someone inside said, "Let 'em in!"

I'd never been in the Walnut Tree before, and not

many people had been in the private room, to judge from the mustiness of it. Mr. Vaughn was seated at a table in the corner. I could only make out his hands and forearms first, lit by a ray of dusty sunshine. His fingertips were resting on the stem of a glass of port wine, and the sunshine passing through the wine cast a shape like a red angel on the table.

"Come closer!" said Mr. Vaughn, in a voice like a boot on wet gravel. "Let's have a look at you."

He was a thin man, with a face that came in from both sides and met sharp in the middle, like a wedge of cheese. His hair was grey and fluffy, his nose was swollen and covered with little purple veins, and his top lip drooped over his bottom lip. He questioned Ma for what must have been close on twenty minutes, but I didn't pay much attention until his watery green eyes flicked from Ma to me.

"Is this the girl?" he asked.

Ma said, "Yes, sir. Matty, sir."

"How old is she?"

"I'm fourteen years old, sir," I piped up.

"And forward too, it seems," said Mr. Vaughn.

I lowered my eyes. "I'm sure I know my place, sir."

Mr. Vaughn leaned forward into the light, so that his head didn't look as if it was connected with the rest of his body. "Tell me, child, are you a Christian?" he said.

"I go to church of a Sunday, sir," I said.

"And are you superstitious?"

"No, sir," I said. "Saving not walking under ladders, and crossing my fingers when a black cat crosses my path."

Mr. Vaughn raised an eyebrow. "Ah! So you don't like cats?" he said.

I didn't know why he was asking me these things, and it made me feel uncomfortable. "I don't care about cats one way or the other, sir," I said, adding quickly, "they're God's creatures, same as other animals."

"Are you highly strung, or given to strange fancies?" said Mr. Vaughn.

For a second I thought that Mr. Vaughn knew about my seeing and a ripple of alarm went through me, then I realized that he couldn't possibly know, and I said, "No, sir."

"For I warn you now that my master, Dr. Hobbes, will have no truck with daydreamers," said Mr. Vaughn. "Do you listen to gossip?"

It was all I could do to stop myself from laughing aloud, for in Little Harding what else was there to listen to but gossip?

"I've been brought up not to believe anything I hear, and only half of what I see, sir," I said.

Mr. Vaughn nodded.

"Good," he said. "You cook, sew, clean and so forth?"

"Quite well, sir," I said.

"Quite well will do," said Mr. Vaughn, "for housework will not be your main concern. Dr. Hobbes has a ten-year-old ward, Miss Catherine. She was the daughter of his niece, and he took her in after her parents died. Dr. Hobbes attends personally to his ward's education, but she requires a companion and playmate. Would that be agreeable to you, Matty Brand?"

I had a feeling then, a prickly sort of feeling. Throughout our conversation, Mr. Vaughn's eyes had bobbed about like a rat trapped in a kitchen. He was keeping something hidden, and all at once I didn't trust him, but I said, "Yes, sir."

Mr. Vaughn smiled.

"Good! Then I am in a position to offer you and your mother employment," he declared. He gave us instructions. A cart would pick us up from the cottage on Sunday morning and drive us to Tagram House, where we would settle in before beginning our duties on Monday.

Once we were outside the Walnut Tree, Ma let out a long sigh of relief.

"Well, my girl!" she said. "We've done well for ourselves and no mistake. Let's go straight home and start packing."

Now that things were settled, Ma was brisk and

busy, but I had an uneasy feeling that I couldn't shake off, and questions I didn't know the answer to.

Why did Mr. Vaughn ask whether I was superstitious, and why was he drinking port so early in the morning?

As we walked back to the cottage, Ma hummed a cheery tune, but I was frowning every step of the way.

Reuben

6

You might think that I was happy to leave Little Harding and all the children who called me names at school, and I suppose that I was happy in a way.

And it was exciting to be taking such a big step up in the world, but I had doubts and worries too. What if I didn't get along with Dr. Hobbes and Miss Catherine? Fretting over this kept me awake most of Saturday night, and when I did manage to drop into a doze, I dreamed that Ma and I had been turned out of Tagram House and were begging in the street.

In the morning I had my usual slice of bread and dripping for breakfast, but it went that claggy in my mouth, it was all I could do to swallow it. I washed it down with milky tea and felt it stick to my insides, a hard lump that wouldn't go away. As I helped Ma wash the dishes, memories of the cottage came back to me. They crept into my mind at first, then they jostled about like a crowd around a market stall. I remembered the time I tripped over the front doorstep and gave myself a scar under the chin that's there to this day, and the old tom cat who used to mark his patch by doing his business on the kitchen window ledge, and Ma blacking the range until it shone like sea-coal. Then I thought of Pa's grave. No one would visit it when Ma and I were gone, which made me feel sad because it was as if we were deserting him, as if he didn't matter to us any more. Ma sensed my sadness and tried to distract me by getting me to imagine what Tagram House looked like, and how many other servants there would be.

A few minutes later we heard the sound of hooves

coming down the lane, and Ma opened the front door just as a horse and trap pulled up on the road outside the cottage. The horse drawing the trap was a chestnut mare with four black socks. A small, wiry man occupied the driver's seat. He wore dark clothes and a little round hat. His face was wrinkled and weather-beaten, the face of a man who spent most of his time outdoors.

"You Mrs. Brand?" he asked Ma.

"I am," Ma told him.

The man looked at me.

"You'll be Mrs. Brand's daughter, I suppose?" he said.

I didn't much care for his tone, which struck me as cocky, so I said, "And who wants to know?"

"Matty!" Ma scolded.

But the man didn't seem to mind.

"You're not backward about coming forward, are you?" he said. "I'm Reuben. I've been sent to fetch you to Tagram House."

Reuben lifted our bags onto the back of the trap,

and me along with them. Ma sat up front beside him. He clicked his tongue, shook the reins, said, "Walk on now, Molly!" and the trap lurched forwards.

For a while there was an awkward sort of silence, then Ma said, "Should I call you Reuben or Mr. Reuben?"

"Can't say as I mind much either way," said Reuben.

"What d'you do at Tagram House, Mr. Reuben?"

"This and that," said Reuben. "Whatever needs doing, I'll lend a hand to."

Then Ma asked the question that I'd been longing for her to ask.

"Tell me, Mr. Reuben," she said, "what sort of master is Dr. Hobbes?"

"One of a kind," replied Reuben. "Locks himself up with his books for days on end and won't talk to nobody. He scribbles away late into the night and walks about muttering to himself. Too much reading and writing can turn a man's wits if he ain't careful."

I didn't know about reading and writing turning people's wits, but Ma had brought me up to respect learning, and I quite envied Dr. Hobbes's being able to shut himself away with books.

"And Miss Catherine, Dr. Hobbes's ward?" I said.

"Pretty little thing, but pale and sickly," declared Reuben. "A dose of opening medicine would do her the world of good."

"What are the other servants like?" I asked.

Reuben threw me a look over his left shoulder.

"Remember what curiosity did to the cat!" he said.

I opened my mouth to apologize, but before I could, Reuben said, "There's Mr. Vaughn for a start."

"We've met Mr. Vaughn. He interviewed us," said Ma.

"Then it must've been in the morning," Reuben said. "Come luncheon, Mr. Vaughn's not much use for anything." Reuben mimed raising a glass to his lips. "Too much of that, if you catch my drift, missus. I'm partial to a drop myself, but Mr. Vaughn's set to drink himself into an early grave."

I knew that Ma disapproved of my hearing talk of this kind, but there was no stopping Reuben once he'd got going.

"Then there's the housekeeper, Mrs. Chivers. Handsome woman, but stern, so it'll pay you to stay on her good side. There's Mrs. Clark, the cook, who's as honest as the day's long and has no more sense than a day-old foal, and Peg, the parlourmaid, who's no better than what she ought to be."

"Does Dr. Hobbes keep a quiet house?" said Ma.

"Mostly," Reuben said. He craned his neck around to look at me. "Don't you pay no heed to the noises," he said.

"Noises?" I said.

"The house has some bad habits and talks to itself of a night, the way that some houses do."

"And what way is that?" I said.

"Why, by sighing and groaning, creaking and knocking," said Reuben. "That's nothing but the water pipes, the floorboards and the foundations settling. It's not so bad in the day, when there's things to do, but at night there are times you could swear someone was walking about."

"Could you?" I said.

I must have looked concerned, for Reuben chuckled as if he'd been teasing me.

"Course, sometimes it *is* someone walking about, for Dr. Hobbes keeps peculiar hours," he said.

That was the last day of the summer. The wind was chill and a faint mist hung in the air. The sky was grey, the fields were green and there wasn't much in between, except church spires and windmills. The road ran beside canals and rivers, and what with the swaying of the trap and the steady clop of Molly's hooves, I slipped into a doze.

I was awoken by a gentle shake from Ma.

"We're here, Matty," she said.

Tagram House was opposite a church, at a crossroads. The grounds were walled off, and screened by lime trees. I could see the house through the main gateway, at the end of a gravel drive that unwound like a steel ribbon. I'd been expecting a palace out of a fairy book, but it was a grey stone house with ivy over the walls, and mullioned windows peering out through the greenery like suspicious eyes. The house wore the ivy like a hooded cloak that it wanted to hide itself under.

I felt a pang of longing, and suddenly the longing seemed to pass through a magnifying glass and concentrate in the spot where someone stood to the left of the house, in front of a tall box hedge. It was a boy with dark hair, wearing a white shirt and black breeches. He had both hands raised to his chest as though he was holding something. For some reason, I thought that he'd found a bird with a broken wing.

"Who's that boy, Mr. Reuben?" I said.

"What boy?"

"The one standing by the hedge."

"I can't see no boy!" Reuben snorted.

I thought Reuben must be teasing me again, and I glanced at him.

"I can't see no one neither!" declared Ma.

I looked back at the box hedge and saw that the boy had gone.

"Probably some local lad, larking about where he shouldn't," said Reuben. "Must've run off when he saw us coming. Just as well he did. The master don't like trespassers."

But I wasn't sure that Reuben was right. The boy hadn't seemed to be on the point of running away. It was more as if he'd deliberately stood out in the open because he *wanted* to be seen.

As the trap rolled through the gateway, I felt just like a trespasser myself, entering a place where I didn't belong and had no right to be.

Mrs. Chivers

Reuben drove the cart around the house to a courtyard. A well stood in one corner with a cast-iron pump set in the top of it. A woman was waiting at the back door, and I knew at once that she must be Mrs. Chivers, the housekeeper.

She was, as Reuben had said, a handsome woman. Her nose was sharp, her hair dark and curly, her eyes were brown and something about their expression reminded me of a hawk. She wore a black silk dress and a white lace cap. Around her waist was a chain-link belt with all the keys of the house dangling from it. She held herself straight and proud, though when Ma and I stepped down from the cart and went to stand before her, her smile seemed friendly enough.

"You are welcome here, Mrs. Brand," she said.

Her voice was almost as deep as a man's, and she spoke proper, without leaving any beginnings or endings off her words.

Ma bobbed her a curtsy and said, "Thank you, Mrs. Chivers, ma'am."

"You had a pleasant journey?"

"Yes, thank you, ma'am."

Mrs. Chivers turned her eyes on me. "Are you hungry, Matty?" she said.

I blushed and mumbled, "A little hungry, Mrs. Chivers, ma'am."

"Then come," said Mrs. Chivers. "I will leave you with Mrs. Clark, while I explain to your mother what her duties will be." She turned and went into the house.

I glanced uncertainly at Ma, who gave me an encouraging smile, and I followed Mrs. Chivers inside.

The back door led into the kitchen passage. We passed the stairs that went down to the cellars, and the door to the sewing room (Mrs. Chivers pointed them out to me) and on into the kitchen.

The kitchen was a steamy fug of delicious smells, sweet and savoury. In the midst of the steam stood a large woman in a white apron. She was round all over, with a bosom like a bolster, and several chins.

"This is our cook, Mrs. Clark," said Mrs. Chivers. "Mrs. Clark, this is Matty, who is to be Miss Catherine's companion. Mrs. Clark will take care of you for the moment, Matty," and she left the cook and me alone together.

"Pleased to meet you, Mrs. Clark," I said.

"Hello, m'dear!" said Mrs. Clark. "Have you come far?"

"From Little Harding," I said.

"That's a fair step, m'dear," said Mrs. Clark. "You

must be famished, a growing girl like you. Can I get you a bite of something?"

"Yes please, Mrs. Clark!" I said.

I spent close to an hour in the kitchen with Mrs. Clark, long enough for me to grow to like her. She was an open-hearted, dithery sort of woman, who told me about her husband, a grocer's assistant, and more about her four sons than I really wanted to know.

When a welcome gap came in her chatter, I said, "Don't you live in Tagram House then, Mrs. Clark?"

Mrs. Clark gave me a look.

"No, m'dear," she said. "We rent a little house in Derlingham. I leave here at eight of an evening, and then I've to be up at five to come back and cook breakfast."

"Isn't that a bother?" I said.

"I don't mind it, m'dear," said Mrs. Clark. "It suits me better that way. I wouldn't spend a night under this roof if you paid me, and that's a fact."

"Why not?" I asked.

"Because—" said Mrs. Clark, and then Mrs. Chivers

returned to the kitchen, and Mrs. Clark closed her mouth so smartly that it made a popping sound.

Mrs. Chivers said, "I'll show you to your room presently, Matty, but first you must have a tour of the house."

There were that many corridors and corners in Tagram House, it was like a maze. As we were walking through the hall on our way to the main stairs, Mrs. Chivers nodded to a door on our left.

"The master's library," she whispered. "You must never go in there unless you are told to, and if you are told to, on no account move anything. The master refers to a great many books and papers in the course of his work, and does not like them to be disturbed."

We climbed up to the turn in the staircase. Judging that we were out of earshot of the library, I said, "What work does the master do, ma'am?"

A strange light shone in Mrs. Chivers's eyes, and when she spoke, it was as if she was reciting a prayer.

"He studies the mystery of life and death," she

said. "One day he will write a great book on the subject, and the world will be changed because of it."

I asked her no more about Dr. Hobbes and his work, for I was sure that all his philosophy and clever ideas were far beyond the likes of a girl from Little Harding. And besides, I was more curious about my new companion.

"When am I to meet Miss Catherine?" I said.

"Not today, I think," said Mrs. Chivers. "She is being tutored by Dr. Hobbes, but the master will see you later this afternoon."

She took me to my room, which was next to Miss Catherine's, with a door that connected the both of them. It was a small room, odd-shaped with a slanty ceiling, which came from it being tucked under the eaves. I had a bed, a little wardrobe and a washstand. On the wall facing the foot of the bed was a tiny window.

"There," said Mrs. Chivers. "Will you be happy here, Matty?"

I was a bit disappointed to be honest, for the room

was almost as small as my bedroom in the cottage. It seemed that living in a big house wasn't so grand once you were actually inside it.

"I hope so, ma'am," I said, keeping my disappointment to myself.

"The door to Miss Catherine's room will be left open during the night, in case she needs you," Mrs. Chivers told me.

"Needs me, ma'am?" I said.

Mrs. Chivers became serious.

"Since the death of her parents, Miss Catherine's sleep is sometimes troubled by nightmares," she said. "She can be a difficult child, given to wild imaginings. Some of what she says may seem strange to you. If you are worried at any time, you are to talk to me about it, but never mention it to anyone else, especially the other servants. Is that clear?"

"Perfectly clear, Mrs. Chivers, ma'am," I said.

There was a bumping and clattering on the landing outside, and Mr. Vaughn suddenly appeared in the doorway of my room. He was in his shirtsleeves, and his collar was unfastened. His hair was tangled into knots, and his bloodshot eyes bulged like the eyes of a frightened horse.

"Did you see, Mrs. Chivers?" he said, his voice skidding over his words. "Did you see the boy, near the rose garden? He was there in broad daylight. I fear he's come back to be revenged on us."

Mrs. Chivers snapped at him like a terrier. "Mr. Vaughn, you are unwell!" she said. "You should return to your room and lie down. What can you be thinking of, roaming about in a state of undress?"

Mr. Vaughn looked down at himself, blinking blearily. "Begging your pardon, ma'am," he mumbled. "I must have a touch of the ague."

But it wasn't any ague, for I'd never known the ague put such a stink on a man's breath. The plain fact was, Mr. Vaughn was as drunk as a lord. Even so, his words made me curious. Was he talking about the same boy that I'd seen, and if so why had the boy come back to seek revenge – revenge for what?

Servants' luncheon was taken in the kitchen – Mr. Vaughn was absent – and it was there that Ma and I met Peg, the parlourmaid. She was fair, with grey eyes and a pert nose, and I guessed her to be seventeen or eighteen years of age. Peg was a pretty girl and knew it, holding her head to one side when she talked to you, and making such a to-do of fluttering her eyelashes that afterwards you couldn't remember the half of what she'd said.

I spent the afternoon in my room, sorting out my bits and pieces. To tell the truth, I had too much time to call my own, and it fair dragged by. I thought about going into Miss Catherine's room, but the door was locked and I didn't know where the key was.

I went to the window and peered out. Down below I saw a garden that was surrounded by hedges. Four paths ran across the lawn, meeting in the centre of a circle of flowerbeds. I'd seen a cross in a circle before, on a monument in St. Stephen's churchyard. The beds here were planted with rose trees. The roses weren't very pleasant to my eye, being a bluey-pinky colour. Because the hedge around it was so high, the garden was mostly in shadow. I couldn't understand why anyone would plant roses in such a gloomy spot. I thought perhaps they might be a special kind that didn't do well in full sunlight, or perhaps the garden wasn't meant to be a rose garden at all, but a garden for growing shadows that could be picked and placed in corners to make them dark.

My imagination ran away with this fancy. I pictured Reuben pottering, squeezing the shadows to see if they were ripe, weeding out the runty ones.

There was a knock at my door.

"Please come in," I said.

It was Mrs. Chivers. "Are you comfortable, Matty?" she said.

"Yes, thank you, ma'am."

"Dr. Hobbes wishes to see you," said Mrs. Chivers.

A shiver ran through me.

"But you are cold!" said Mrs. Chivers. "You are trembling."

"I'm sorry I'm sure, ma'am," I said. "I'm not at all cold. That's just nerves, that is."

"There's nothing to be afraid of, Matty," said Mrs. Chivers. "I'm sure you'll meet with Dr. Hobbes's approval."

I wasn't sure. I followed Mrs. Chivers downstairs to the library, with dread perched like a pirate's parrot on my shoulder, and my heart pounding. I didn't know whether it was because I was in awe of the great scholar, or whether there was something more to my fear. When Mrs. Chivers opened the library door, I lowered my eyes and stepped inside.

Mrs. Chivers said, "Here is the new girl, Dr. Hobbes – Matty Brand."

And I looked up.

The First Night

The library was a shambles. Books were jammed higgledy-piggledy on the shelves, stacked in rickety piles on the floors, and papers were scattered everywhere.

Then I saw Doctor Hobbes seated at a desk. The world seemed to vanish like a raindrop sinking into dry ground, and there was only me and him, and no one else mattered. He looked like a saint in a stained-glass window, and for all the whiteness of his hair, his skin was as smooth as a child's. His nose was straight, with a bit of a hook to it, and there was a dimple in his chin, but his eyes were his most striking feature. They were as blue as circles of summer sky, and they had a way of pulling you down deep into them that was downright uncanny.

A quiver ran up and down my back, and I could only hope that Dr. Hobbes didn't notice it.

"I'm sorry that I didn't greet you earlier, Matty," he said. "Catherine and I forgot about the time."

His voice was deep, and as rich and brown as gravy.

"I'm pleased to meet you, sir," I said, tipping him a little curtsy.

"Have you been well looked after since you arrived?" said Dr. Hobbes.

"Oh yes, sir," I said.

"I'm glad to hear it," Dr. Hobbes said with a smile. "I understand that you're a local girl."

"Little Harding born and bred, sir."

Dr. Hobbes raised his eyebrows. "An interesting spot for those who study history. You know St. Stephen's Church, of course."

"I do, sir," I said.

"Then you must have noticed the three tall stones in the churchyard wall."

"Yes, sir," I said. "They're called Long Tom, Sarah and Nicodemus."

"Have you ever wondered how those stones came to be where they are?"

I knew the story went that in the time of King Alfred, the parish priest had tricked the Devil into carrying the stones to the church, but I remembered Mr. Vaughn warning me that Dr. Hobbes didn't hold with superstition, and I said, "No, sir."

"They were raised as a temple by Ancient Britons who worshipped the sun and the moon," said Dr. Hobbes. "Little Harding was one of the places where the old beliefs hung on long after the first Christian missionaries had done their work. So a church was built, and the stones were made part of the churchyard wall, and the ancient religion was forgotten."

"Thank you for enlightening me, sir," I said, using a long word in hopes that it would impress him.

"I think that you and Catherine will get along," said Dr. Hobbes, "but you must be patient with her. She is an unusual child. I'm afraid that there are times when she finds it difficult to tell the difference between what she has imagined, and what has actually taken place."

"I'll do my best to be a good companion to her, sir," I said.

"I'm sure you will," said Dr. Hobbes. "I sense that you have a strong spirit, Matty, and those who have a strong spirit may achieve anything that they put their minds to. But have a care, for strong-minded people sometimes turn stubborn, and when that happens, they must be broken."

As he spoke, a steely edge seemed to enter his voice, like a knife cutting through his silky tones. He clenched his fist, and looked me so directly in the eyes that I blushed as though I'd been caught doing something wrong.

"That will be all for the present, Matty," said Dr. Hobbes. "I look forward to speaking with you again."

Mrs. Chivers was waiting for me in the hall.

"There now, Matty, I told you that you had nothing to fear," she said with a smile. "The master is charming, isn't he?"

"Yes, ma'am," I said.

Dr. Hobbes had been thoroughly charming, but I'd glimpsed something else in him, something that I didn't quite understand, but knew it would be dangerous to provoke.

I wish I had a magic red-hot poker that could burn out the memory of my first night in Tagram House, for it's so clear in my mind that I can still taste and smell it.

I went to bed at nine o'clock. I'd heard it said that folk didn't sleep well for the first night in a strange place, but I must have been too tired to remember this, because I went to sleep almost as soon as I'd blown out my candle. The sleep didn't prove to be peaceful though, for in the dead of night I was woken up by scrabbling noises overhead. At first I thought there must be mice in the attic, then I heard footsteps and whispering. I couldn't make out any words, but a burst of giggles made me certain that it was children up to mischief.

They must have broken in, I thought to myself. I should fetch Mr. Vaughn.

I sat up to get out of bed, and a new noise turned me as still as a statue. It was a splintering, scraping sound, like strong claws scratching at rough wood. I was sure someone, or something, was trying to dig through the ceiling to get me.

I didn't know whether to stay, run, or call out for help – and then I did call out, for the door that connected my room to Miss Catherine's sprang open, and I saw a figure holding a lighted candle in a candlestick. The figure wore a long white shift, like a funeral shroud. Its face was lit from beneath by the fluttering candle flame and hardly looked human. It was framed in billows of black hair, and its dark eyes stared wildly.

"W-who are you?" I said, my voice shaking with the thudding of my heart. "What d'you want?"

"I'm lost Catherine," said the figure.

I heaved a huge sigh of relief. "You frightened me, Miss Catherine," I said. "Whatever are you doing out of your bed at this hour – did the noises wake you?"

"What noises?" said Catherine.

And she was quite right, for when I listened I found that the noises had stopped.

"I woke up because the Dragon Man was in my room," Catherine went on.

"The Dragon Man?" I said. "Who's the Dragon Man?"

"He flies through the night, stealing away sleeping children."

"There's no Dragon Man," I said. "That was just a nasty dream. Shall I take you back to bed and tuck you in?"

Catherine looked horrified. "No!" she said. "I won't go back in there. I won't, I won't!"

I could tell a tantrum was brewing.

"Hush, or you'll wake everybody," I said. "What a fuss for a big girl like you to make about a silly dream."

I called her "a big girl", but to tell the truth she was tiny, as skinny as a stair-rod, and she looked far younger than her ten years.

Catherine came closer, and held out the candle so that its light shone on my face.

"Are you my new companion?" she asked.

"Yes, Miss Catherine," I said. "I'm Matty."

"I like that name," said Catherine. "When will you leave?"

"Not for a long, long time."

Catherine shook her head; her hair rustled against the shoulders of her shift.

"No," she said. "You should leave as soon as you can."

"Why, don't you want us to be friends?"

"I have friends," said Catherine.

"So many that you can't be doing with another?" I said.

Catherine sat down on the edge of my bed.

"Where do you go when you're asleep?" she asked.

"Nowhere I can't get back from in time for morning," I told her.

"I go to a dark place underground," said Catherine. "It smells mouldy. I can feel people walking on top of me, but I can't tell them to go away because my mouth is full of mud."

I didn't know what to say to her, she seemed too young and delicate to have such horrible thoughts, and she was frightening me.

"I'm cold," said Catherine. "Can I get into your bed?"

"I don't know about that," I said. "Whatever would Mrs. Chivers think?"

In a surprisingly hard voice, Catherine said, "Mrs. Chivers may think what she likes!"

"That's not a very kind thing to say," I said.

"I'm not a very kind person," said Catherine. "I don't know how to be."

"If you're not kind to other people, they won't be kind to you," I said.

"Will you be kind to me?" said Catherine.

"Why, of course I will!"

"Then it would be kind of you to let me into your bed."

She had me there, good and proper. I drew back the covers and said, "Come along then. Mind you blow out your candle first."

Darkness fell. The bed moved as Catherine wriggled in and pressed herself against me.

"You're as cold as the grave!" I said, and straight away I wished that I hadn't, for I thought I might have reminded her of her dead parents.

"And you're warm," said Catherine. "I'm safe now."

"Good. Go back to sleep and dream about the fairies."

"Fairies," said Catherine, "are the folk memories of spirits that were once supposed to inhabit springs and forests."

"Are they?" I said. "Then dream about kittens instead."

Catherine snuggled in to my back, and before long her breathing became heavy.

"Don't die," she mumbled drowsily.

I didn't reply, thinking that she wasn't talking to me, but to a dream.

I stayed awake for a while in case the scratching and whispering came back. I wondered if they were part of what Reuben had meant when he'd told me about the house talking to itself at night. But all stayed quiet overhead, and eventually I fell into a deep sleep.

The Toy Chest

I've never been one to lie around in bed in the morning. I always think that if the sun's up and about then so should I be, and I generally wake early. But Catherine beat me to it the next morning, for when I opened my eyes she was leaning up on her elbow, gazing at me. She didn't seem so strange by daylight, except for her eyes. They were old beyond her years, and I thought that all the tears she'd cried for her parents must have aged them.

"You'll know me if you see me again," I said. "Don't

you know it's not polite for young ladies to stare?"

Catherine poked her tongue between her lips, blew hard and made a *most* unladylike sound.

"I don't give a fig for what young ladies do!" she said. "You're younger than my last companion. Her name was Elspeth. I was fond of her, but she didn't stay for long. We had to send her away."

"Why was that?"

"She became deranged and had to be taken to an insane asylum," Catherine said. "This house was too much for her."

I thought that this must be something that she had imagined, and I smiled as if she'd made a joke.

"You're a tease!" I said. "You're making up stories to frighten me."

"Am I?"

"You know you are. Well, I won't be frightened, so don't you try."

Catherine frowned anxiously and said, "If I grow fond of you, will it make you deranged as well?"

"I should say not!" I snorted. "I'm a country girl,

plain and simple. I keep my feet on the ground and my head out of the clouds."

Though I protested loudly, what Catherine had said made me uneasy, for I knew I wasn't as plain and simple as I'd made out and some people would think that a girl who claimed to see the spirits of the dead was deranged already.

"Oh, you're not plain!" said Catherine. "You're as pretty as pretty can be." She reached out to touch my face and as she did the sleeve of her nightdress slipped back, and I saw a line of scars on the inside of her arm, some silvery with age, others dark and new.

"Goodness, Miss Catherine!" I cried. "Whatever have you been doing to yourself?"

"Nothing," said Catherine, hurriedly pulling the sleeve down to her wrist.

"Then what are all those cuts?"

Her expression changed to a look that didn't belong on a child's face.

"If you must know, it's for my own good," Catherine said. "There are times when I'm not quite myself, and I need to have my blood let. My guardian bleeds me in his study. He mixes me a special drink to calm me and waits until I'm feeling soft and dreamy. Then he sits me down in an armchair and takes a little silver bowl and a silver knife that's sharper than a razor. When he cuts me, I hardly feel it. He collects the blood in the bowl and covers it with a fresh white linen cloth so that I don't see it. Afterwards he cleans and binds the wound and mixes me a cup of hot chocolate, and I'm better."

I was properly flummoxed and no mistake. How much was true and how much was Catherine's imagination I had no way of telling, but I thought that if Dr. Hobbes bled her then she must need bleeding, or else why would he do it? Even so, it seemed an old-fashioned way of treating someone, and it made me shudder to think of it.

So my life at Tagram House began and the days soon settled into a routine. I had breakfast, luncheon and tea with Catherine in the schoolroom, which had obviously once been a playroom, for as well as a pair of desks and chairs, and shelves of books there was a large rocking horse. During the mornings I would read to Catherine, listen to her reading aloud and test her understanding by asking her questions. After luncheon, if the weather was fine, we walked in the grounds for an hour or so. After tea, Catherine went to the master's study for her lessons and took supper with him. My supper was taken with the other servants. Catherine was an affectionate girl and mostly happy, though there were times when she was tired and tetchy. I grew accustomed to her, and then attached to her. In the hours that we weren't together, I helped Mrs. Clark in the kitchen, and Ma would generally find some time to meet me and talk, though she worked so hard that I didn't see her that much.

Night-time was a different matter. As soon as the sun set, a change came over Tagram House. Rooms that had been warm and cosy all day grew draughty.

Corridors would suddenly turn so cold that I could see my breath on the air. Reuben had warned Ma and me that the house was noisy at night, and so it was. Lying in my bed I heard all kinds of trudging footsteps, creaking and groaning, and more than once a sorrowful sigh that made me want to get up and give comfort to the poor soul who had heaved it. I didn't dare, of course, because I was afraid that it might be Dr. Hobbes, pacing the house at night the way that Reuben had told me he often did. What comfort could a girl from Little Harding give to a learned man like him?

One evening after Mrs. Clark had gone home and Catherine was with her guardian, I became restless and decided to tidy the schoolroom. There wasn't much tidying to do, just a few books that Catherine and I had left lying about, and I thought that while I was putting them away I might as well rearrange the volumes on the shelves in alphabetical order. It was dark so I took a lighted candle with me. There was a gas light in the room, but we'd never had gas at home and I was afraid that I might blow myself up if I tried to use it.

It didn't take me more than ten minutes to tidy up the books, and my restlessness was no better. I looked about and noticed for the first time that what I'd taken to be a window seat at the far end of the room was in fact a wooden chest covered by a cloth. A corner of the cloth had been pulled back, exposing the lid of the chest. Even though I knew that I had no business to, boredom and curiosity got the better of me, and I couldn't resist having a look inside.

The chest was filled with toys that I assumed were Catherine's: a china doll in a splendid dress and hat, so clean that it couldn't have been played with very often; a tattered rag doll that seemed better loved; a board and a set of draughts. Then further down I found a popgun, a bow and arrows, and a tin battleship on wheels. These didn't seem right for a young girl like Catherine.

I was still puzzling when a stern voice behind me said, "What are you doing, Matty?"

I was so startled I almost screamed. I turned my head and saw Mrs. Chivers standing in the doorway.

"Please, Mrs. Chivers," I said quietly, "I was just going through these things."

"Put them back into the chest," commanded Mrs. Chivers.

She sounded so angry that I was certain she suspected me of thieving, so I said, "I wasn't going to take anything, ma'am. I'd never do anything like that."

Mrs. Chivers's face softened a little.

"I know you wouldn't," she said. "You're an honest girl, Matty, but you must not pry into matters which do not concern you."

I couldn't understand why she was so angry, but I did as I was told.

When I picked up the battleship a thought occurred to me and I said, "Mrs. Chivers, have other children been at Tagram House?"

I saw her flinch, but when she spoke her voice was calm and even.

"What makes you ask that?" she said.

"Some of these are boys' toys, aren't they? And there are two desks in the room."

Mrs. Chivers hesitated before she answered.

"Yes, there were other children here some years ago – Guido and Bella," she said. "They were brother and sister. Reuben found them sheltering in the grounds after they had been abandoned by their vagabond parents."

"Guido and Bella," I murmured. "They're foreign names, aren't they?"

"The parents were Italian. They had a travelling puppet show, or something of that sort," said Mrs. Chivers. "The master took the children in out of the goodness of his heart and gave them every comfort, but in the end they treated him very badly indeed. After they had been here a few months, they ran off with a large sum of money and a set of silver spoons."

"How ungrateful!" I exclaimed. "Did Dr. Hobbes send for the constable?"

"Indeed he did, but no trace of the children was ever found." A sour smile played on Mrs. Chivers's lips. "Whether that was a result of their cunning, or a failure on the part of the constabulary is not for me to say. The master was upset by the incident and does not care to be reminded of it."

"Then why did he keep the toys?" I murmured to myself.

"Hurry up, Matty!" Mrs. Chivers urged. "It's almost time for you to go down for your supper."

She watched until I put away the last of the toys, then stepped back onto the landing.

I followed her. Just as I was closing the door, I saw – or thought I saw – something flit among the shadows in the far corner of the room. I raised my candle to cast light into the corner, but it revealed nothing but the glints in the rocking horse's glass eyes.

"Don't dawdle, Matty," said Mrs. Chivers. "Your supper will be going cold."

The Schoolroom

10

That night I had a dream that seemed real, a dream that's stayed with me ever since.

I dreamed that I was lying in bed, waiting to fall asleep, when I heard a tapping on my window, a thin sound like pins dropping into a glass. I told myself it must be rain and tried to ignore it, but the tapping was insistent. It kept on and on until I couldn't stand it any longer. I threw back my sheets and blankets, went to the window, and as I drew back the curtain the tapping stopped.

It couldn't have been rain that I'd heard, for the sky was clear and starry, with a big moon that shone down into the shadow garden, making the paths and bushes silver. A sudden movement caught my eye, and all at once a young girl in a white nightgown walked into the garden. She had long dark hair and a face as pale as moths' wings.

I was certain that the girl was Catherine and that she was in great danger. Panic drove me from my room and out onto the landing. I moved so silently through the house that I seemed to be gliding, and when I reached the back door, its bolts pulled themselves back, and it opened without a sound. I crossed the threshold into the night.

Real fear came to me then, and gripped my innards with icy fingers. More than anything I didn't want to go into the shadow garden, but my concern for Catherine forced me to go on. I walked around the side of the house and followed the path that led to an archway cut into one of the box hedges that surrounded the garden. There I paused.

The young girl was standing just where I'd seen her, but she wasn't Catherine. Her hair was as dark and long as Catherine's, but it was straighter and silkier, and her face was rounder. She stared at me, her arms crossed over her chest and her palms pressed to her shoulders, like the Egyptian mummy I'd once seen a picture of in a history book.

Just then I had a feeling that was strange, even for a dream. The girl was wrong somehow. She didn't fit in the shadow garden, or the night, or the world.

"Who are you?" I said. "What d'you want?"

The girl replied by lowering her arms.

The top of her nightgown was black with dried blood from a wound that ran from her throat to her waist.

I suppose I should have been horrified or disgusted, but instead I was sad. Though she said nothing, I knew that the girl wanted me to pity her and I did, so strongly that tears welled up in my eyes.

"Who did this to you?" I whispered.

The girl pointed down at her feet, and the whole shadow garden fell away from me as fast as a stone dropping down a well –

And I woke up.

Ma used to tell me that nightmares were a sign of a guilty conscience, but I couldn't remember doing anything that would make me guilty enough to deserve the nightmare that I'd just had.

The dream was still with me as I washed and dressed, but I tried to put it out of my mind, though it had left me feeling tired out. I went down to the kitchen as usual to collect a breakfast tray from Mrs. Clark, while Catherine was being dressed by Peg. I carefully carried the tray upstairs to the schoolroom where Catherine and I always took breakfast together, but when I opened the door I almost dropped the lot.

The room had been wrecked. The desks had been overturned and one of the chairs was smashed. Books lay scattered like broken birds. The toy chest had been emptied out and its contents trampled. The once proud head of the china doll was shattered, the bows and arrows were snapped and the tin battleship was flattened.

Still holding the tray, I backed out of the room and almost bumped into Mr. Vaughn, who was on his way downstairs.

"Watch where you're going, girl!" said Mr. Vaughn.

Words tumbled out of my mouth, like falling dominoes.

"Oh, Mr. Vaughn, sir!" I said. "Something awful's happened, and I don't know what's to be done, and it wasn't my fault, really it wasn't!"

Mr. Vaughn was wearing his morning face. His eyes were as baggy as a bloodhound's, and all squinnied up as though the light was too bright for them.

"What are you prattling about?" he said gruffly.

"Why, the schoolroom, sir," I said.

Mr. Vaughn strode past me and went to look for himself. He took a sharp breath, and his eyes opened so wide that I almost heard them pop.

"Merciful heavens!" he croaked.

"Who could've done it, Mr. Vaughn?" I said. "Who'd be so nasty as to—?"

Mr. Vaughn held up a hand to silence me. Some kind of struggle seemed to be going on inside him, and he shook from head to foot. He reached into his jacket and took out a metal hip flask that he uncorked and raised to his lips. I heard his teeth rattle against the neck of the flask, and I caught a whiff of strong liquor.

Mr. Vaughn put the flask back into his jacket and cleared his throat.

"Tidy up as best you can, Matty," he said.

"Will you send someone to fetch the local constable, sir?" I asked.

Mr. Vaughn's reaction surprised me, for he laughed.

"A fat lot of use the constable would be in circumstances like these!" he said bitterly.

"Circumstances like what, Mr. Vaughn? Surely, if a burglar has —?"

Mr. Vaughn glared at me.

"Open your eyes, girl!" he snapped. "I locked the door of this room at ten o'clock last night and I unlocked it barely half an hour ago. Do you see any signs of forced entry or broken windows? And has anything been stolen?"

"I haven't looked, sir," I said.

"Take my word for it, nothing has been stolen," said Mr. Vaughn.

There was something in his voice that made me ask, "Mr. Vaughn, has this kind of thing happened before?"

Mr. Vaughn said, as though to himself, "I must tell Mrs. Chivers about this right away," and he went off leaving my question unanswered.

It didn't take me long to straighten the schoolroom, and Catherine's breakfast was still warm when she arrived. I decided not to alarm her by informing her about the break-in, and we passed the morning reading picture books and telling each other stories. Shortly before lunch, Peg came to the schoolroom with the message that Dr. Hobbes wanted to see me in the drawing room.

"What for?" I said, alarmed.

Peg sniffed, rolled her eyes in a disdainful way and said, "How would I know? The master don't discuss his business with me."

"Was he annoyed when he spoke to you?"

"He wasn't nothing," said Peg. "I'd get a move on if I were you, he don't like to be kept waiting. I'm to look after Miss Catherine while you're gone."

Catherine's expression of delight at this news gave me a pang of jealousy.

"I was telling Miss Catherine the story of—" I said.

Peg interrupted me with a sneer. "I know what kind of stories Miss Catherine likes," she said.

On my way downstairs, I was stung by a swarm of worries. Did Dr. Hobbes think that I'd wrecked the schoolroom? Was he going to turn out Ma and me, and where would we go if he did?

I knocked on the door of the drawing room and heard Dr. Hobbes say, "Come in."

He was standing by the window, light streaming through his hair. He had been seated behind his desk at our last meeting, and I was surprised now by how tall he was and how powerful he seemed.

"Good afternoon, Matty," he said. "Please take a seat."

He waved his hand towards a chair and I sat down.

"Have you recovered from your unpleasant discovery this morning?" Dr. Hobbes continued.

"Yes, thank you, sir," I said.

"I'm glad to hear it, Matty." Dr. Hobbes frowned and shook his head. "I must admit that the matter has greatly disturbed me. An attack on my property is tantamount to an attack on myself."

"Whoever would want to attack you, sir?" I gasped.

A look of sadness came into Dr. Hobbes's face.

"Did you know that once there were two other children at Tagram House, Matty?" he said.

"Mrs. Chivers told me, sir," I said. "They were called Guido and Bella."

"Guido and Bella!" Dr. Hobbes said with a sigh. "I believe that they were responsible for the damage to the schoolroom."

He paused as though he were weighing something in his mind. At last he said, "Have you noticed anything out of the ordinary recently, Matty? Have you encountered any strangers about the place?"

I thought of the noises at night and my terrible nightmare of the girl in the shadow garden, but I feared that if I spoke of them, Dr. Hobbes would accuse me of being fanciful.

"No, sir," I said.

"You're quite sure?"

"Yes, sir."

Dr. Hobbes seemed satisfied with this.

"Very well," he said. "I would be obliged if you would say nothing about the schoolroom to anyone except myself, Mrs. Chivers or Mr. Vaughn, and should you notice anything unusual, please let one of us know at once."

"I shall, sir," I said.

Dr. Hobbes stroked his chin.

"If Guido and Bella have returned to the vicinity, they may well be planning more mischief," he said.

"Did they steal any keys, sir?" I said.

"Keys?" said Dr. Hobbes, frowning.

"If they had keys they could have let themselves into the house and the schoolroom without forcing any locks or windows," I said.

"Keys," Dr. Hobbes muttered. "Yes – yes indeed."

He seemed distracted. His gaze was fixed on the rose garden outside the window, and he appeared to forget that anyone else was in the room.

I could tell that the interview was over, so without being dismissed, I crept out and closed the door as quietly as I could to avoid disturbing the master. But I was deeply puzzled. Something didn't seem right somehow, but I couldn't quite put my finger on what it was.

The Walk

11

Though Ma and I saw each other every day, we didn't get much chance to talk on our own. Most of our private chatting was squeezed into our walk to and from Sunday morning service at St. Luke's, the church across the way from Tagram House. It's not like Ma or me were very religious, but it was a comfort to hear the old familiar prayers and to sing the same hymns that we'd sung at St. Stephen's.

We were given one afternoon a month off, and at

first we managed to spend the time together, but in November, shortly after the wrecking of the schoolroom, I had a free afternoon, while Ma's free afternoon was set for the following week.

It was Friday, a dank day with an overcast sky, but I didn't mind the dull weather. I had made plans for that afternoon, and I wasn't going to change them for anything.

I'd heard that Tagram House was very near the coast, and though I knew the sea from picture books at school, I'd never seen it in real life. Was it as wide as people said? Was it true that the waves changed colour and never stopped moving? I longed to know, and I was determined to take a walk and find out for myself.

I had lunch with Catherine, then she followed me up to my room and watched sulkily as I put on my overcoat and gloves.

"If you're only going for a walk, why shouldn't I come with you?" she said, maungy-like.

"You see enough of me as it is," I said. "There

are times a body needs to be by herself to think her own thoughts. It'll do me good, and it'll do you good too."

This wasn't strictly the case. Fond as I was of Catherine, I wanted to be on my own for my first sight of the ocean, and I needed to think over my bewildering conversation with Dr. Hobbes.

Catherine pouted.

"It's not fair!" she grumbled. "I'll be alone and bored."

"You know that's not true. Peg will be with you," I said. "You like Peg."

"Yes, but not as much as I like you," said Catherine. A cunning look came into her eyes. "Peg tells me things that I'm not sure I should know," she said.

"Oh – what kind of things?"

Catherine shrugged her left shoulder.

"About life, and fashion, and what sweethearts do," she said.

There wasn't much that I would have put past Peg, but I suspected that Catherine was fibbing.

"And what *do* sweethearts do?" I asked.

"Why, don't you know?" said Catherine. "Take me with you and I'll explain all about it."

"You'll do no such thing," I said. "You won't twist me around your little finger that easily."

Catherine's sulk changed into a fit of temper, and she stamped her foot.

"Go on your stupid walk!" she shouted. "You can get lost and never come back for all I care!"

And with that she stormed out of the room.

I was a bit taken aback. Catherine usually spoke in such a grown-up way and had such grown-up ideas, that when she behaved like the little girl she actually was, it came as a surprise.

"You'll have to find a way of making up with her later, Matty Brand," I told myself.

I left the house by the back door, which was only proper for a servant, and as I made my way around the side, I heard someone singing a song. I couldn't make out the words and the song didn't have much of a tune, just the same note over and over. The voice was coming from the shadow garden, and I went to investigate. Since my bad dream I'd kept well away from the place, but I knew I'd have to get the better of my fear sooner or later, and now seemed as good a time as any. I passed through the arch, prepared for anything, but there was no nightmare waiting, only Reuben, who had his back to me.

I almost laughed because Reuben was acting so oddly. He was shaking powder out of a small leather pouch in his left hand, while his right hand drew circles and spirals in the air, and his feet shuffled in a clumsy dance.

"Whatever are you doing, Reuben?" I said.

Reuben stiffened and scowled at me over his shoulder.

"I'm getting the garden ready," he said.

"Ready for what?"

"The winter," Reuben replied. "I'm singing the roses to sleep."

"Singing the roses to sleep?" I giggled. "I never heard of such a thing."

Reuben turned to face me.

"I don't expect you have, seeing as how you come from Little Harding," he said, "but this is how we do it round here. My pa taught me the trick of it. If I don't sing the roses to sleep, they might wake up before spring, and then where would we be, eh?"

"I'm sure I don't know."

"No," Reuben agreed, "and I'm sure you don't know as well."

"What are you sprinkling on the ground?" I enquired.

Reuben gripped the pouch more tightly, as though he was afraid that I might snatch it from him.

"It's a special recipe, handed down from father to son through generation after generation. It helps to settle things that ought to be asleep, roused-up things that ought to be quiet."

I didn't understand him. I couldn't be sure if he was teasing me again.

"You'd better not let Dr. Hobbes catch you," I said. "He doesn't approve of superstitions."

"What the master don't know won't hurt him," said Reuben.

"Why was a rose garden planted in such a gloomy spot?" I asked curiously.

This was one question too many for Reuben.

"For the same reason you can't keep your beak out of other folks' doings!" he said gruffly. "Now clear off and let me get on with my work."

I turned away though I was still puzzled and more than a little alarmed. Reuben's strange antics had done nothing to dispel my fear of the shadow garden. More than ever it seemed to be a place of mystery and dark secrets.

Once I was outside the main gate, I turned right along the Derlingham road. The countryside around Tagram House wasn't very interesting because it all looked the same: flat fields bounded by hedges, stands of trees and the occasional farmhouse.

As I walked along I brooded on my talk with Dr. Hobbes. When he'd told me that Guido and Bella wanted to harm him, I'd accepted it without question. But now I wondered why they wanted to harm him when he'd shown nothing but kindness towards them. I suspected there was far more to it, and that Dr. Hobbes had kept things from me.

After a mile or so I reached a track that joined the road like a stream running into a river, and I followed it on impulse. It ran through a hawthorn thicket, then into a little wood of fir trees with blue-green needles and small brown cones. I heard a faint hissing sound and there was a taste of salt on my lips. At the edge of the wood the ground sloped away, and I found myself looking at a wide sandy beach. The tide was out and the distant sea was as grey as slate. The stretch and space of it made me catch my breath, and all my doubts and worries were blown away by the wind.

In a kind of trance I stepped onto the soft sand

and idly drifted towards the tideline. The sand beneath my feet firmed up and I noticed that seashells lay scattered all around me. When I saw a pretty one, I picked it up and put it in my pocket as a present for Catherine.

Time went away, as it can do when you've only yourself for company, or perhaps I went away, but don't ask me where. The next thing I remember is being close to the edge of the sea, watching long waves roll themselves into foam. Seagulls yelped and screamed above me, and their crying turned into the voices of sailors and fisherman crying for help, some speaking in languages that I couldn't understand. Their drowned voices were drowning me.

I covered my ears with my hands, turned to face the land and the voices fell silent, as if a door had been slammed on them. I could see the wood I'd walked through, and there, standing at the edge of the trees and staring back at me were two children, a boy and a girl, both with long dark hair.

I don't know what put it into my head that the

children were Guido and Bella, but I was suddenly certain of it. A surge of feelings broke over me like one of the sea's cold waves. I felt loss, and ache, and loneliness, and something wrong that only I could put right.

"I'm coming!" I shouted. "Wait there!" And I ran, with the wind pulling at my coat so that its tails flapped like wings. The beach was as wrinkled and ridged as a tree trunk. I stumbled, almost fell over, and lost sight of the children. When I reached the spot where I'd seen them standing, I couldn't find any trace that they'd been there, though I searched the wood for a good half hour. The only footprints I came across were my own.

At first my thoughts ran as wild as children in a playground, but then I forced myself to calm down. Why would Guido and Bella follow me to such a deserted spot? They were interested in Dr. Hobbes, not a serving-girl from Little Harding. Most likely the children had been locals who'd been frightened off by the shouting mad girl charging at them. The lack of footprints only meant that the sand was too soft to hold clear tracks.

I told myself that I was being ridiculous; I told myself everything but the truth.

Hob

12

I didn't tell anyone about what happened on the beach. I would've sounded like a silly country girl who let her imagination run away with her. So I kept it to myself – one more secret among all the other secrets in Tagram House.

The following afternoon, the master sent for Catherine a good hour earlier than usual, and I was left with time on my hands. I went down to the kitchen to offer my help to Mrs. Clark, and also in hopes of catching the chance of a few words with

Ma. Mrs. Clark was glad of my company, and while she saw to the making of tea and supper, I washed up pots, pans and dishes.

I knew Mrs. Clark pretty well by this time. She was a dear sort and I liked her – but Lor', how she could talk. She chattered away like a flock of sparrows in a holly tree. There was no end to her stories and gossip, and I don't think she was ever one to let the truth get in the way of a good yarn. Her gossip was harmless and mostly about people I didn't know, so I didn't pay much attention.

Among the washing up I had to do was a big carving knife. I left it for last because it was wickedly sharp and I was afraid that I might lose it in the soapy water and cut myself by accident. I'd put the knife to one side of the draining board to keep it separate, but when I reached out for it, it wasn't there. I lifted plates off the drying rack to see if the knife had slipped underneath, but it hadn't, so I bent over to peer at the floor.

"Is something wrong, m'dear?" said Mrs. Clark.

"I've lost the carving knife," I said. "It was here a moment ago, but it's gone."

"Ah!" Mrs. Clark said knowingly. "He must be up to his old tricks again."

"Who?"

Mrs. Clark blushed, and her eyes hopped about like magpies.

"No one!" she said. "It's all stupid nonsense."

"What is?" I asked.

Mrs. Clark's voice dropped to a murmur.

"The master don't like such talk, and I'd be in ever so much trouble if you repeated what I'm about to say, but it's my opinion that there's a hob in this house," she said.

"What's a hob?" I said.

"A sort of sprite," said Mrs. Clark. "If a hob takes a fancy to a place, he'll move into it and do little chores – dusting and cleaning and whatnot. I once heard of a dairymaid who made a pet of a hob, and he used to churn her butter for her overnight, and it was the best butter in the county. Hobs are generally kind, but they're cranky and easily offended. If you don't treat 'em right they turn nasty and play pranks, such as hiding away a thing when you've most need of it."

For a moment I thought Mrs. Clark must be joking, but her expression was deadly serious.

"And what makes you think there's a hob in Tagram House?" I said.

"Well, so many things have gone missing and turned up again where they were least expected," said Mrs. Clark. "I remember one time, not long after I came to work here, that I dropped a skewer. I heard it hit the floor, but when I looked I couldn't find it, though I searched high and low. You'll never guess where I found it in the end."

"Where?"

"When I was getting ready to go home, I saw that skewer pinned through my hat, right where it had no business to be, looking as strange as strange," said Mrs. Clark. "If that wasn't a hob's work, whose work was it, I should like to know?"

"Perhaps one of the other servants played a trick on you," I said.

"But how could they, when I was here by myself?" said Mrs. Clark. "And who'd do such a thing? Mrs. Chivers and Mr. Vaughn aren't the trick-playing kind, are they?"

"It might have been Reuben – or Peg," I suggested.

"No," said Mrs. Clark. "Reuben didn't come anywhere near the house that day, and Peg saves all her tricks for good-looking young lads."

"Could it have been Elspeth?" I said, remembering Catherine's talk of her previous companion.

The expression in Mrs. Clark's eyes was so sad that I was sorry I'd asked.

"Not her, poor soul!" she said with a sigh. "There are those who aren't long for this world, and I reckon she was one."

"What became of her?" I said.

"She was a shy little thing," said Mrs. Clark. "Her family was well-to-do, but they fell on hard times. Miss Elspeth tried to fit in with us servants, but you could tell that she was used to better ways than ours. The only person she really talked to was Miss Catherine. Heaven knows how she loved the child – loved her until it was a kind of sickness that addled her brains. She accused the master of all sorts, and one day she attacked him with a hammer she'd stolen from Reuben's tool shed. Mr. Vaughn and Mrs. Chivers held her down and tied her up. A policeman was fetched, then doctors, then Miss Elspeth was taken away to the county asylum."

So Catherine *wasn't* fibbing, I thought.

Mrs. Clark shook her head as if she was trying to shake away unpleasant memories.

"The hob's been quiet for a long while, but something's got his dander up," she said. "I'll have to leave out a saucer of milk and a slice of cake in the pantry."

Mrs. Clark had been so honest with me about the hob that I was tempted to confide in her about what had happened to me at the beach, but just then Ma came in with a load of dirty dusters for boiling in the copper in the scullery. She didn't stay more than a couple of minutes, but the moment had passed. Mrs. Clark was busy at the stove and I didn't have the courage to tell her about my imaginings. I kept thinking about Elspeth and her madness... Was the same thing happening to me?

That night, before I went to bed, I listened at Catherine's door to make sure that she was sleeping soundly. Then I undressed, put on my nightgown and kneeled beside my bed to say my prayers.

"Lord bless and keep me," I whispered, "and Ma, and Miss Catherine, and Dr. Hobbes, and—"

At that moment there was a loud thump on my door. I opened my eyes and looked across the room.

An icy draught blew over me, and the flame of my candle burned blue. Its ghastly light made my hands look as though they belonged to a waxwork.

I stood up, went to the door and said, "Who's there?"

The silence outside mocked me.

Terrified though I was, I seized the door handle, turned it and wrenched the door open.

There was no one to be seen on the landing, but the carving knife I'd misplaced in the kitchen earlier in the day was stuck into my door at a point level with my waist. The knife hadn't been driven very far into the wood, for as I stared at it in bewilderment it fell to the floor with a clatter. I snatched it up, stepped back into the room, closed the door, turned the key in the lock and stood trembling.

Someone or something was playing a game with me, and I didn't like it one bit.

I didn't sleep properly after that, only managing to doze fitfully. My mind wouldn't leave the knife alone. How could it have got from the kitchen to my bedroom door? How could anyone have taken it without being noticed by me or Mrs. Clark? I began to think that she was right about the hob, and it gave me a crawly feeling to think I was sharing a house with a sprite.

What with puzzling and not sleeping, my thoughts

were as twisted up as a bramble patch. I kept picturing Mr. Vaughn finding the knife in my room and accusing me of stealing it. To calm my fear, I crept down to the kitchen at daybreak and slipped the knife back into the cutlery drawer.

On the way back, I came across a further puzzle, for as I walked along the landing, I heard voices coming from Catherine's room. Catherine laughed, and then her laughter was followed by a voice that I didn't recognize. But when I stopped outside the door, the room was silent.

Imagining things again, Matty Brand? I thought. You're so tired you can't tell whether it's Christmas or Easter.

And I shuffled off to my bed to find what sleep I could. I was glad that the sun was rising and that the night was at an end, for I'd found out that Tagram House could do more than just talk to itself during the hours of darkness.

friends

13

Next morning at breakfast, Catherine behaved as if she hadn't slept any better than I had. She yawned widely, poured far too much milk into her bowl of porridge and then stared at it as if she didn't know what it was.

"You'd best eat that up before it goes cold," I said.

"I'm not hungry," said Catherine.

"It's a shame to waste food," I said. "There's plenty who'd be grateful for a breakfast like yours."

Catherine pushed the bowl away from her.

"Well let them eat it!" she snapped.

"Who's a little crosspatch this morning?" I said. "Did you have a bad dream last night?"

"No."

"Then why did I hear you talking to yourself in your room in the early hours?" I said.

Catherine sniffed haughtily.

"I wasn't talking to myself, I was talking to my friends," she said.

"What friends?"

"My special friends," said Catherine. "Sometimes they play with me, though I don't much like their games."

"And you let them in your room at night?" I said.

Catherine smiled.

"I don't *let* them in my room, they just turn up there," she said. "They're good at getting into places, and they're especially good at hiding. They visit me when no one else is near. They grow out of the shadows."

Catherine's tone of voice reminded me of the way

she had spoken about the Dragon Man on my first night at Tagram House, and I felt a twinge of anxiety. Was she fibbing, or were her friends part of the strange behaviour and morbid thoughts that Dr. Hobbes and Mrs. Chivers had mentioned? Could they be connected to the flitting shadow I'd seen in the schoolroom? I looked deep in Catherine's dark eyes, but there was no spark of mischief in them. As far as I could tell she was speaking the truth, and I wanted to find out more.

"So," I said slowly, "in a way your friends are there, but in another way they're not – not like you and I are here now."

Catherine clapped her hands in delight.

"That's exactly right!" she exclaimed. "You are clever, Matty. My friends think so too."

"Very kind of them, I'm sure," I said. "Do they have names?"

Catherine nodded.

"Their names are Guido and Bella," she said.

Goodness only knows how I managed to get through breakfast without letting on to Catherine how alarmed I was. I smiled until my face ached and talked who-knows-what nonsense, but all the while my mind was spinning round like a cartwheel. When Peg appeared to collect the dishes, I asked her to stay with Catherine, and I rushed off in search of Mrs. Chivers.

I found her in the drawing room, where she was writing in a thick book. She appeared to be more interested in her writing than in me, but when I blurted out what Catherine had told me, she put down her pen and listened. Her expression became more and more serious.

"Please, ma'am, we should search the house at once!" I said at last. "Guido and Bella are hiding somewhere. I'm afraid that wrecking the schoolroom wasn't enough mischief for them, and they mean to get back at Dr. Hobbes by doing Miss Catherine an injury."

"Come, come, Matty," said Mrs. Chivers. "You

aren't thinking clearly. Tagram House is large, I agree, but not large enough for two children to come and go without being noticed."

She leaned forward in her chair.

"Miss Catherine was without a companion for several months," she said. "It's more than likely that she invented friends for herself, as lonely children often do. She must have overheard someone talking about Guido and Bella – most likely Mrs. Clark or Reuben – and took their names for her imaginary playmates."

"But Dr. Hobbes told me that he thought Guido and Bella were responsible for the damage in the schoolroom," I said.

Mrs. Chivers pursed her lips and appeared to think hard for several moments. When she spoke again her voice was grave.

"Dr. Hobbes was protecting Miss Catherine – and you – from a terrible truth," she said. "You genuinely care for Miss Catherine, don't you, Matty?"

"Yes indeed, ma'am," I said.

"Then I think that I can trust you with the truth, but you must keep it strictly to yourself – understand?"

"Yes, ma'am."

Mrs. Chivers folded her hands in her lap.

"Miss Catherine has unfortunately inherited a nervous condition from her father," she said. "It's a rare condition, for which medical science has yet to discover a cure. For the most part Miss Catherine is normal and healthy, but when her condition flares up she loses control of herself. When this happens, it's vitally important that she is restrained, or the nervous inflammation might spread to her brain, and the consequences of that would be fatal."

My heart sank.

"Can't anything be done, ma'am?" I asked.

"Dr. Hobbes is treating Miss Catherine personally and does what he can to soothe her when she is overwrought. Like you, he is deeply fond of her, but he can't be with her all the time," said Mrs. Chivers. "It seems that, acting under the influence of her condition, Miss Catherine vandalized the schoolroom and lost all memory of it afterwards. You must watch her carefully. This talk of Guido and Bella may simply be a childish fantasy, or a warning sign that she is about to have another seizure."

I shuddered. I'd heard tell of people having seizures, of how they fall down, foaming at the mouth, thrashing their arms and legs, and biting their tongues clean in two. The thought of such a thing happening to Catherine turned my insides over.

"Oh, Mrs. Chivers!" I groaned. "Whatever shall I do if Miss Catherine has a seizure when we're on our own together?"

"You'll be brave and strong, and keep your wits about you for her sake," said Mrs. Chivers. "If Miss Catherine has a fit, get help from me, Mr. Vaughn or Reuben, whoever is closest to hand."

"Miss Catherine will get better one day, won't she, ma'am?" I said.

The sad look on Mrs. Chivers's face told me more than her words did.

"All we can do for Miss Catherine is to look after her for as long as Fate allows," she said.

I remembered how Catherine had once called herself "lost Catherine", and now I thought that I knew the reason why.

"I'll do everything I can to protect her, ma'am," I vowed.

"I know you will," said Mrs. Chivers. "Miss Catherine is fortunate to have a companion as loyal as you, Matty. I'm sure that if you're tested, you won't be found wanting."

As things fell out, I was tested far sooner than I expected, and Mrs. Chivers's warning had come not a day too soon.

Haunted

I returned to the schoolroom, where Catherine and Peg were sitting side by side on the toy chest, whispering to each other. All at once Catherine threw back her head and laughed.

I had a powerful feeling then. The sound of Catherine's laughter made me want to scoop her up in my arms and whisk her off to a place where nothing bad could ever happen to her. If I'd known how, I would have struck a bargain with God or the Devil to give me her illness and her my good health. It seemed to be awful that her life might be cut short while so many wicked people would live on into old age.

Peg slipped off the chest, straightened her pinafore and patted her hair.

"I was just saying to Miss Catherine what a shame it is to be shut indoors on a morning like this," she said. "Young girls need plenty of fresh air and exercise."

I wondered what had suddenly made Peg such an expert, but I stopped myself from saying something sarcastic and peeped out of the window. I hadn't noticed the morning until then, but it was lovely. The sky was pale blue and the sunlight was the colour of cider.

"Peg's right," said Catherine. "Oh, please take me for a walk, Matty! It'll be winter soon and I shan't be able to go out, and besides, my head is so full of dust that I'll be sneezing cobwebs any minute."

Her pleading look would have melted an anvil, and how could I have said no to her after learning what I'd just learned?

"All right," I said, "but wrap up warm. I think the weather's colder than it looks."

🍂

Down in the entrance hall, I helped Catherine into her grey overcoat. She put on a plaid tam-o'-shanter cap and wound a long, blood-red scarf around her neck.

"Don't forget your gloves," I said.

"I won't," said Catherine. "What will you wear?"

I unhooked an old-fashioned hooded cloak from the hall stand.

"This'll do me," I said, swirling the cloak over my shoulders. "Country girls like me don't feel the cold. We're used to it."

Catherine regarded me for a second or two.

"You look like a girl from a story book," she declared at last. "I wouldn't be surprised if a handsome young prince fell in love with you."

"I hope not!" I gasped. "I wouldn't know what to do with a handsome young prince if I met one."

"I suppose you'd canoodle with him, as if he were an ordinary young man," said Catherine.

I laughed.

"That's enough of that sort of talk," I said. "If Mrs. Chivers heard us talking this way, she'd hand me my notice."

And I bustled Catherine outside.

There was no warmth in the sun, and the easterly breeze was bitter.

"Where shall we go?" said Catherine.

She was inviting me to play a game that we often played on our walks, pretending that we were visiting different parts of the world.

"India?" I suggested.

"No," said Catherine. "India is too far away, and we might be eaten by tigers."

"London?"

"London is too near, too crowded and too dirty," said Catherine. "Let's walk as far as the fountain and pretend that we're in Italy."

The fountain was in the middle of the front lawn.

It was an ugly great stone thing, shaped like a gigantic scallop shell, with sea creatures that spouted water from their gaping jaws. There were no water jets that morning though. The fountain had been turned off to prevent the frost from freezing its pipes, and the scallop shell was coated with dried mud and dead leaves.

"Italy is a beautiful country," said Catherine. "The weather is warm. You can pick oranges and lemons straight from the trees, and grapes from the vines. If it gets too hot, you can shelter in the shade of an olive grove." She stood in front of the fountain. "Look, Matty!" she said. "This is the famous Trevi Fountain in the heart of Rome. They say that if you close your eyes and throw a coin over your shoulder into the fountain, you're bound to visit the city again."

"You know a lot about Italy," I said admiringly.

"Yes I do," said Catherine. "Some friends of mine described it to me."

"Guido and Bella?" I said.

Catherine nodded and began to walk slowly around the fountain.

"I don't mind playing the Italian game with them," she said, "but I don't like the other game."

"What other game?" I asked.

"The still game," said Catherine. "You have to lie down on your back with your arms at your sides and stay there, without moving, until all your breath leaves you and everything goes dark. You can hear the sound of the earth in the dark, and feel blades of grass growing out of you, and the world forgets that you were ever born."

"That doesn't sound much fun," I said.

"Guido and Bella don't play games for fun," said Catherine.

I wondered if Dr. Hobbes knew about Catherine's imaginary friends, and if the knowledge might help him to understand more about her condition.

"Have you told Dr. Hobbes about Guido and Bella?" I said.

Catherine scowled.

"Of course not, silly!" she said. "That wouldn't do at all. He'd kick up an awful fuss."

"Why, because Guido and Bella aren't real?" I said.

"Because of the *way* they aren't real," said Catherine. "My guardian doesn't understand these things like you do. He wants to explain the world in a book, and he leaves out what can't be explained."

"Have you told Mrs. Chivers?" I said.

"Mrs. Chivers?" Catherine said scornfully. "That woman's nothing but a –"

I didn't understand what Catherine said next for she spoke in a foreign language, and something about her had changed. Her eyes were blank and her voice seemed different.

"Catherine, stop it!" I shouted.

Catherine looked at me and her eyes suddenly focused again. She turned and ran laughing towards the house. I followed, convinced that she was either having a fit, or was about to have one. Instead of running directly to the front porch, she veered off to the left, and I knew with deadly certainty that she was going to the shadow garden.

I was out of breath and on the edge of panic when I caught up with Catherine in the middle of those awful rose beds. She was standing quite still, and I saw her eyes roll back until the whites showed.

Two figures appeared in front of her, as suddenly and miraculously as a picture from a magic lantern jumping onto a screen, a girl and a boy, both with long dark hair. The girl was the girl from my nightmare. She wore the same clothes, though thankfully there was no wound on her chest. The boy wore a white shirt and black breeches, like the boy I'd seen on my first day at Tagram House. They gazed at me with deep imploring eyes.

Sadness coursed through me. These children had no one else but me to mourn for them. I knew exactly who and what they were – Catherine's playmates were the spirits of Guido and Bella.

And then I realized something else too. These spirits were drawing strength from me, just as poor

Sammy Byers had drained my strength all those years before. My energy waned and I felt weary.

Guido was pointing at Catherine, and Bella held her hands together, as if in prayer.

They didn't seem to want to hurt Catherine, as I'd feared. They were pleading with me, warning me.

"I'll protect her!" I blurted, without knowing that I had been going to say it.

Guido smiled – such a pitiful smile that I almost wept – and then the two spirits vanished.

Catherine stumbled against me. I held her close and whispered, "There, now. You're safe," though the words sounded hollow to my ears for I feared that she was anything but safe.

I was dazed and shaken but one thing was clear enough: Mrs. Chivers had been mistaken. Catherine wasn't suffering from any nervous condition: she was haunted.

A Dream Embrace

15

Catherine went slack in my arms. She breathed evenly, perfectly still for a moment before wriggling.

"I don't mind being held, but I wish you'd do it more gently, Matty," she said.

"Sorry," I said, and let her go.

Catherine took a step back, and when I saw her face it shook me harder than anything else that had happened. Just a few seconds before she'd been like a girl under a spell. Now she seemed as right as raindrops.

"I don't like this garden," she said, glancing around. "I think it's sad. I wish you hadn't brought me here, Matty."

A cat could have knocked me down with a twitch of its whisker.

"Brought you here?" I gasped.

"You ran in here when we were playing tag just now, and I followed you," said Catherine. "You could have chosen somewhere more cheerful."

What was she talking about? I had followed *her* into the garden.

Didn't she remember Guido and Bella appearing just now? Had they taken away her memory? I wasn't sure what was going on, but I knew for certain that spirits who walked in this world were not happy spirits, and their warnings were not to be ignored.

"You look cold!" said Catherine. "Let's go inside at once and toast crumpets at the fire."

❧

Lord only knows how I managed to get through the rest of that day. I forced myself to stay calm and acted as if everything was normal, though inside I was as tangled up as a kitten in a sewing basket.

By rights I ought to have gone straight to Mrs. Chivers and told her about Catherine's outburst. I'd given Mrs. Chivers my word and I felt guilty for not keeping it, but something held me back. Mrs. Chivers would never accept that Catherine was being haunted, and was sure to put it down to her illness. If I tried to explain the truth, Ma and I would most likely be turned out of Tagram House. So I jammed a tight lid on the truth, though the lid rattled as the truth threatened to boil up and spill over.

That evening, while Catherine was being taught by Dr. Hobbes, I went looking for Ma. She was in the kitchen, laying out the cutlery for the servants' supper. Mrs. Clark had already left for home, so I had Ma to myself.

"I've got to talk to you, Ma!" I said.

Ma smiled.

"You are talking to me, Matty," she said. "What's got you in a lather?"

I lowered my voice.

"Not here," I said. "We're servants here. After supper, let's go outside, where we can be ourselves. Meet me in the shadow garden."

Ma gave me a puzzled look.

"The rose garden," I said. "It'll be quiet there."

If you'd asked me then and there why I'd chosen the shadow garden, I wouldn't have been able to tell you. Now, looking back, I wonder if I was being guided – or would "drawn" be a better word?

Ma put on her stern face.

"Have you got yourself into trouble, Matty?" she demanded.

"No, Ma," I told her. "At least, not yet, anyway."

Supper seemed to drag on and on. I had no idea what the food I was putting in my mouth tasted like, and everything appeared peculiar and threatening, from

Peg's sly glances to Reuben's thin smile. It was as if the other servants were in the know about something and had me just where they wanted me. Even the air seemed to turn against me, and my skin shrank from it.

The end of the meal came as a relief. After I'd helped to clear the dishes away, I tried to slip away without being seen, but Peg spotted me and smirked in that aggravating way of hers.

"Off out, Matty?" she said.

"Yes, not that it's any of your business," I said.

Peg narrowed her eyes, tilted back her head and looked down her nose at me.

"Going to meet your sweetheart, are you?" she teased.

"No, and you shouldn't judge people by your own standards," I said, coming over all prim and hoity-toity.

Peg laughed at this, which was no less than I deserved.

It was cruel cold that night, with stars throbbing

away in the black sky, and enough of a moon to see by. The greeny-gold gas lights in the windows of the house looked so welcoming that I almost changed my mind and turned back, but then I remembered Guido pointing at Catherine, and I strode around the house to the shadow garden.

Ma was already there, pacing about to try and stay warm, and clutching a grey woollen shawl that was draped over her shoulders.

"Whatever it is, make it short, Matty," she said testily. "If we stay out too long we're liable to catch our deaths."

So I told her straight out about the schoolroom, the beach, the walk to the fountain. Only I couldn't get it right. It sounded like a lot of fibs.

When I'd finished, Ma groaned and twisted her fingers in the shawl.

"Oh, Matty!" she sighed. "Why d'you have to go and see things everywhere? There was I thinking that good luck had come our way at last, and now this."

"I can't help it, Ma," I protested.

"More's the pity," said Ma, "and you won't learn to forget what you've seen and keep quiet about it neither."

"What should I do, Ma?" I pleaded.

"You must do what you've always done, Matty, keep your secrets to yourself," said Ma. "If Dr. Hobbes or Mrs. Chivers hears you talking about ghosts, we'll be out on our ears."

"But I want to help Miss Catherine!" I cried.

"It doesn't sound to me as if she needs your help," said Ma. "You don't think the spirits mean her any harm, do you?"

"No," I admitted. "But I think somebody does."

"Don't worry, Matty," Ma said more gently. "They'll turn out the same as all the other spirits. Bide your time and they'll go away of their own accord."

"But—"

"Never you mind no buts," said Ma. "Just bide your time."

And since this was the only advice available to me, I took it.

That night I had a dream that was strange, happy and sad mixed together into one. I dreamed I was in St. Stephen's churchyard, standing next to Pa's grave. There was a man standing opposite me. He wore labourer's clothes, and his big hands were rough, with chipped and dirty nails.

"I've a message for you, girl," the man said. "Have a care. It ain't what it seems, not none of it. The kind are wicked, the strong are weak, and you're in danger. If you won't run, you'll have to stand and fight. Trust no one but yourself, d'you hear me? No one."

I didn't much like being ordered about by a stranger.

"Who are you?" I said, offended-like.

The man's face softened.

"Why, don't you know your own father, Matty Brand?" he said softly.

And then I saw that he *was* Pa, for he looked exactly like me with all the bits of Ma taken out of my face.

"Pa?" I said. "Oh, you don't know how I've missed talking to you!"

"About as much as I've missed being talked to, I reckon," Pa said. "But you ain't got long with me, so listen careful-like. Them foreign childers were about ready to give up. They thought that little Catherine girl was their last hope, and they couldn't get her to do anything more than play. They were about ready to drift away like smoke, when you came along and gave 'em new pep. They're happy that someone's listening at last."

"I'm listening, but what are they telling me?" I said.

"That your business is among the living, not the dead," said Pa. "That's where you'll find your answers, Matty." He looked around. "It's coming on dawn," he said.

Then I did something that I'd been longing to do

for as long as I could remember. I jumped over the grave, into Pa's arms, and he held me. His embrace was that safe, I didn't want to leave it.

"Don't let me go!" I said.

"Never!" promised Pa. "Whether you see me or not, I'll always be holding you, my girl."

A chill wind blew around my neck and tugged at me.

"You got to go now, Matty," said Pa.

I woke with an ache in my throat, and my eyeballs prickling with uncried tears. I lay still, holding on to the feeling of the dream embrace until it died away and I was on my own.

The Shed

16

Just before sunrise Catherine appeared in my room, holding a book and demanding that I read her a story. She looked so wistful and vulnerable that I couldn't refuse her, so I made space for her in my bed and lit a candle.

The book was *The Wonder Book of Yarns for Girls and Boys*.

"Which story shall I read?" I asked.

"*The Little Match Girl* by Hans Andersen," Catherine replied. "Elspeth was very fond of it, and

I haven't heard it for ever so long."

I found the story, read it out loud and at the end, when the starving girl froze to death on the city street, I was appalled.

What kind of tale is that to tell children? I thought to myself.

But Catherine was fascinated.

"Will the match girl be happy in heaven with the angels and her grandmother?" she asked.

"She's sure to be happy," I said. "Heaven is where God and Jesus live."

"Perhaps," Catherine said with a shrug.

"What d'you mean – *perhaps*?" I said.

Catherine drew up her knees and wrapped her arms around them.

"The God of the Bible isn't the only god," she declared. "He says so himself."

"Does he?" I said, astonished.

"Yes, in the Old Testament," said Catherine. "The First Commandment says, 'Thou shalt have no other gods before me', which only makes sense if there *are* other gods for people to worship. My guardian has explained it all to me."

Sunday school lessons at St. Stephen's hadn't prepared me for anything like this, and besides I didn't like Catherine's haughty tone. I drove away Miss Know-It-All the best way I knew how, by tickling her until she was red-faced and panting, and a little girl again.

That was the Catherine who was most dear to me, and I tried to imagine a rosy future for her, a future where she grew into a beauty, married a handsome young man and lived happily ever after in a fine house.

The room had grown light, making the candle flame into a faint ghost of itself.

"*La mattina!*" announced Catherine.

"Beg pardon?" I said.

"*La mattina,*" Catherine repeated. "It's Italian for *morning.* Guido and Bella taught me how to say it."

A shadow fell across the bright future that I'd glimpsed. I remembered what Pa had said about finding answers among the living, so as casually as possible, I asked, "Who told you about Guido and Bella?"

Catherine giggled.

"Why, they told me themselves, you silly," she said.

"But someone must have mentioned them to you before that, surely?"

Catherine's gaze was glassy, and her voice seemed to come from far off.

"Reuben," she murmured. "Reuben knows."

Footsteps clumped along the landing.

Catherine's eyes cleared, and she wrinkled her nose.

"Bother!" she snapped. "That's Peg come to tell me that my bath is ready. Baths can be disagreeable, can't they?"

"Not as disagreeable as being dirty and smelly," I said.

And it was at that moment, when Catherine was most herself, that I made up my mind. I had to protect this waif-like girl from whatever it was that was threatening her. I had to find out what Reuben knew and get to the bottom of the mystery of Guido and Bella.

On my way to collect a breakfast tray from the kitchen, I met Mrs. Chivers at the foot of the stairs.

"Ah, Matty!" she said. "I was coming to find you. Once Miss Catherine has finished her breakfast, please send her down to the library. Dr. Hobbes has to attend to some business in Norwich, and he wishes to take Miss Catherine with him."

"Very well, ma'am," I said with a nod.

"Dr. Hobbes has booked rooms at the White Lion Inn," Mrs. Chivers continued. "Peg will pack Miss Catherine's bag. Would you be so good as to carry it down into the hall?"

"Indeed, ma'am," I said.

I was relieved, for this turn of events fitted in nicely with my plans. Catherine would be safely out of the way with Dr. Hobbes, and while she was away in Norwich I would be free to find out what I could about Guido and Bella.

Over breakfast, Catherine was that excited and chattered so that she could hardly keep her food in her mouth.

"Have you been to Norwich, Matty?" she asked, spraying me with muffin crumbs.

"No," I said. "The biggest town I've ever been to is Coombholt, and I was so little that I can't remember it."

"There'll be lots of shops, I'm sure – and perhaps a department store," said Catherine. "Do you think I'll take a ride in a motor car? Oh, I do hope so! My guardian says that he's going to buy me new clothes and take me out to high tea."

"You'll be quite the grown-up," I said.

Catherine frowned.

"I wish you were coming too, Matty," she sighed. "I'm grateful to Dr. Hobbes, but I'll have to be on my best behaviour while I'm with him. If you were there, it would be more fun."

"Go on with you!" I chided. "What would a gawk of a country girl like me do in a place like Norwich? I'd knock over the tea things, put my thumb in the cream jug and get run down by a motor car, likely as not."

Catherine giggled, then became serious.

"I do hope that Dr. Hobbes won't have to bleed me while we're away," she said. "I don't like being bled very much, and I sometimes wonder how I can have any blood left in me."

I felt a pang of sympathy. There was no denying how tired and worn Catherine looked. She was like a pressed flower whose colour faded a little more each day.

"I'm sure he's only trying to help you," I said.

"I know," Catherine admitted reluctantly. "I really should be more grateful for being such a lucky girl. I have no idea why Dr. Hobbes chose me rather than one of the other children in the orphanage, but I'm glad that he did."

"But I thought –" I faltered.

"You thought what, Matty?"

"That you and Dr. Hobbes were related," I said.

"Oh, who knows?" Catherine said airily. "No one tells me anything. Relative or no, he's a generous man, and I *love* trying on new clothes."

She sounded so shamelessly vain and selfish that I couldn't resist giving her a hug.

"Reuben knows," Catherine had told me, and I was eager to find out what it was that Reuben knew, though my eagerness would have to keep until he returned from driving Dr. Hobbes and Catherine to Derlingham station. In the meantime I tidied the schoolroom, peeled some vegetables for Mrs. Clark and then I went outside. Once again I felt the pull of the shadow garden, but this time I was determined to ignore it, so I walked past the tall hedges to explore the gardens that lay beyond.

Everything was cut back, tied down and thinned out for winter. The only flowers in bloom were

Michaelmas daisies, and their yellow and lilac looked sickly against the bare earth. I've always loved the fiery leaves of autumn and the white sharpness of winter, but the weeks between the two, when it's neither one season nor the other, is a dank slimy time, the colour of a toad's back.

I came to a door in a stone wall that was green with moss. Above the door a dark swag of ivy hung down like a scowling eyebrow. I had often seen Reuben pass through this door, but had never ventured beyond it myself. I turned the ring of the door handle and heard the latch snick as it lifted.

The door opened onto a walled garden, divided into beds by lines of bricks. Plants had been trained up three of the walls, and a lean-to shed had been built against the fourth. I guessed that this was Reuben's den, his workroom and storeroom, hidden away from the prying eyes of the house. I tried to peep in through the shed's single window, but the glass was so thick with dust and cobwebs that I couldn't see anything. However, the door had been left unlocked, and it creaked open at my touch. I stood on the threshold and peered in.

There were shelves of earthenware pots, a rack of rusty tools, a broken whetstone, a row of jars. I was disappointed. There were no secrets here, just a gardener's bits and bobs. I was about to turn away, when it struck me that the jars were labelled with names that I didn't recognize as plant names – Adder's Mouth, Hare's Eye, Mother's Heart. Behind the labels were dried leaves, packed tightly together.

Then I noticed the red circle that had been painted on the floor, and the charcoal drawing on the wall facing me. At first I thought the drawing was meant to be a stag reared up on its hind legs, but as I stared more closely, I saw that the deer had human hands and feet instead of hooves.

What secrets had Reuben shut away behind these walls within walls? If Catherine was right, the secrets might well be linked to Guido and Bella. All spirits wanted to rest after death, and those that couldn't had good reasons for their restlessness, mainly because death had snatched them away before they'd had a chance to live properly. Poor Sammy Byers had been taken by illness. Others came to more violent ends. Was that it? Had something dreadful happened to Guido and Bella? That would explain the ghastly wound I'd seen in Bella's chest the night I dreamed of her.

My thoughts were racing. Had Guido and Bella been murdered?

Hobnails grated on the gravel behind me.

"What d'you think you're doing?" rasped an angry voice.

A Talk in the Walled Garden

17

I'd never seen Reuben so furious. There were red spots on his cheeks and little flecks of foam at the corners of his mouth.

Playground fights had taught me that attacking was sometimes the best way to defend myself, so before Reuben could say another word, I laid into him.

"How dare you come sneaking up behind me that way, Reuben!" I scolded. "You almost frightened me out of my wits. If you went lurking and skulking round Mrs. Chivers like that, you'd get a roasting for certain sure."

Reuben was taken aback and wilted slightly.

"I'm no sneak and I don't skulk neither," he said. "You got no business poking around my shed."

"*Your* shed?" I hooted. "So this must be your garden and your house too, I suppose? Well, your lordship, for your information I haven't been poking around your precious shed. I looked inside to see if you were there, that's all."

"Did you touch anything?" Reuben asked suspiciously.

"There's nothing in that shed that's clean enough for me to touch," I said. "Did you see Dr. Hobbes and Miss Catherine onto the Norwich train?"

Reuben opened his mouth to reply, then growled.

"That ain't got nothing to do with nothing!" he said. "What the Devil you want me for, anyway?"

I took a deep breath to steady myself.

"I want to find out more about Guido and Bella,"

I said, "and Miss Catherine told me that you might be able to help."

Reuben jerked as if someone had dropped an icicle down his back. His cheeks lost their redness, and he lowered his eyes.

"What'd she say that for?" he mumbled. "I don't know no more than what anyone else does."

"Not according to Miss Catherine," I insisted.

Reuben scratched the back of his head and fiddled with the woollen muffler that was wound around his neck.

"They were foreign, Eye-talian," he said. "You couldn't understand the half of what they were saying. They jabbered away to each other like a pair of monkeys."

"What were they like?" I said.

Reuben moved his left hand as if he was trying to pluck words out of the air.

"Girl was pretty enough, a bit slow on the uptake," he said. "The boy was a varmint. Sly eyes, he had, like a weasel's. If there was any mischief going, he'd be in on it somewhere. When I heard as they'd stolen money and run off, I wasn't surprised."

"Did you ever see them again afterwards?" I said.

Reuben took his time about answering.

"Not exactly," he said eventually. "Not the way you mean, any road."

He was trying to wrong-foot me.

"In what way then?" I said.

"There's times things come back when they shouldn't," said Reuben. "Times when they're not wanted."

This reminded me of what he'd said about making things sleep the morning I found him singing in the shadow garden.

"What sort of things?" I said.

Reuben's sly smirk made his eyes crinkle at the edges, and suddenly he was the oldest person I'd ever seen, with a face as seamed and withered as perished leather.

"If you've got to ask me that question, you'll never understand the answer to it," he said.

Reuben didn't think that I knew what he meant, but I knew very well. He was talking about ghosts, and the ghosts of Guido and Bella in particular. I still didn't quite understand his strange dance in the rose garden, or the things painted in his shed, but it was as plain as plain that there was more to Reuben than the rambling country bumpkin he pretended to be. He was something stronger, something as weird and ancient as the thing that sometimes used my eyes to see with.

"Get along about your work, Matty Brand, and leave me be about mine!" Reuben said in a surly voice.

As I walked away from the walled garden, I thought hard. Was Reuben at the heart of the mystery of Tagram House? Guido and Bella had begged me to protect Catherine – could it be Reuben who was threatening her? Was he responsible for the deaths of Guido and Bella?

Black, threatening questions flocked like crows in my mind.

The Return

The next day dawned grey and gusty. Blasts of wind bent the trees and sent their stripped leaves tumbling across the lawns of Tagram House. The eaves moaned, the wind hooted and whistled in the fireplaces until the air seemed filled with lonely voices and sad songs.

As Catherine was still in Norwich, I took breakfast in the kitchen with the other servants, but their company wasn't much comfort. Mr. Vaughn was watery-eyed and grumpily silent. Peg preened as she inspected her reflection in the bowl of a spoon. Ma was as nervous as a mouse, eating in quick nibbles and darting off as soon as she'd done.

"Your mother's in a hurry this morning," remarked Peg. "Is something worrying her?"

"Why should there be?" I replied angrily, though I knew Peg was right. Ma was nervous these days, worried that I might let slip something about the things I'd seen.

Peg smiled, enjoying my annoyance.

"Who got out of bed the wrong side then?" she said. "Not so full of yourself when Miss Catherine isn't here for you to hide behind, are you?"

"Shut your row, Peg!" growled Mr. Vaughn. "Your blasted chitter-chatter would try the patience of a saint."

"Which you're not!" Peg muttered saucily.

"What's that?" said Mr. Vaughn.

Peg batted her eyelids.

"I asked if your tea was still hot, Mr. Vaughn, sir," she said. She tipped me a wink, but when I didn't respond she flounced off to go about her duties.

I waited in the kitchen until the others had gone, and helped Mrs. Clark to wash the dishes. This wasn't out of the kindness of my heart. I wanted to know more about Reuben, and I judged her to be my best source of information. As usual, she was full of her family, and I let her talk her fill about her husband and sons.

When she fell quiet – well, quiet for Mrs. Clark – I said, "How long have you worked here, Mrs. Clark?"

She blew air over her face to move a strand of hair that had fallen across her eyes.

"Best part of four years now," she said.

"And how long has Reuben been here?"

Mrs. Clark shook her head.

"Who knows?" she said. "I sometimes reckon that Reuben's been here longer than the house. He was here before the master's time, that's for sure."

"He's got some funny decorations in that hut of his," I said. "There's a red circle on the floor and—"

Mrs. Clark almost dropped the soapy plate in her hands.

"You didn't ought to go near that shed, Matty, and you shouldn't speak of what you find there!" she interrupted.

"Why not?"

Mrs. Clark clutched my arm and drew me close so that I could catch her whisper.

"Reuben's a wise man," she said.

"Reuben – wise?" I said doubtfully.

"He's wise in the ways of plants and animals," explained Mrs. Clark. "Knows his herbs, does Reuben, and a charm or two to help things along."

"D'you mean magic?"

"I mean that Reuben's a true countryman," said Mrs. Clark. "Time was that every village had its wise man or wise woman, but those days are dead and gone."

"Does Dr. Hobbes know?" I demanded. "Or Mr. Vaughn, or Mrs. Chivers?"

"In this house we keep what we know to

ourselves," said Mrs. Clark, "and you'd best do the same. Least said, soonest mended."

Though I wondered what had broken that needed mending, I said nothing because I could tell that the subject was closed. But though my voice was still, my brain was humming like a hive. I was convinced that Reuben's strange singing had been a spell intended to get rid of the ghosts of Guido and Bella. Were they haunting him because of his part in their deaths? I had to stop him before he hurt Catherine too, and the only way I could think to do that was to tell Dr. Hobbes all I knew. It didn't matter that he might be angry and send me and Ma packing – Catherine's safety was more important than anything else.

If only I'd known then what I know now, I would have seen that my racing thoughts were carrying me down completely the wrong road.

Catherine got her wish to ride in a motor car, but not in the way she had expected.

It must have been about two o'clock that afternoon – not long after lunch. I was in the back court with Ma. We'd strung out a line between two hooks, draped rugs over the line, and we were thrashing away with a pair of carpet beaters. Dust came out of the rugs in grey puffs, like a horse's breath on a frosty morning.

Then all of a sudden came a shrieking and hawing that made the hairs on my arms stand up. Later on I learned it was the sound of a car's horn, but I hadn't heard one before, and in my imagination I saw a rusty iron donkey, braying for all it was worth.

Voices called out urgently.

Ma and I went indoors to see what the to-do was about and hurried through to the front hall. The door was open, and I could see a car parked outside, a great silver thing with headlamps that glared, and a snarling radiator. The driver was seated behind the wheel, a plump man wearing a grey overcoat, a flat cap with the peak turned around to the back and a pair of motoring goggles that gave him a froggy look.

I took in all this in a brief glance, for after my eyes fixed themselves on Dr. Hobbes, I couldn't tear them away.

His silver hair was windblown, and his eyes were as bright as blue fire. Catherine lay in his arms, wrapped in a dark blanket. Her head lolled and her hair trailed down. Her face was grey and her eyes were closed.

For a moment I thought that Catherine was dead, and something seemed to trip over inside me, but then I saw her fingers twitch and her lips part. The moan she made was no louder than the mewling of a kitten.

"Stand aside!" commanded Dr. Hobbes. "Bring hot-water bottles and brandy."

And he carried Catherine upstairs.

I wanted to go to Catherine, but each time I tried someone stopped me. In the end, Mr. Vaughn ordered me to stay in the kitchen, out of the way. I did as he told me, though I called him a few names under my breath.

As the afternoon wore on into twilight, I could feel anxiety eating me up. The worst part was not knowing. I gathered bits and bobs from Ma and Peg as they came and went, but they didn't add up to much. Catherine had been taken ill in Norwich, they said, so ill that Dr. Hobbes had hired a car and a driver to bring her back to Tagram House because it was quicker than returning by train.

At last Mrs. Chivers appeared in the kitchen and asked for me.

"The master wishes to speak with you in the library, Matty," she said.

I followed her into the passage, and she paused for a moment to put her hand on my shoulder.

"You must be brave, Matty," she said.

I was going to be brave all right, brave enough to tell Dr. Hobbes the truth about Reuben.

A fire had been lit in the study. The master was seated in front of it in a worn leather armchair. He gave no sign of noticing that anyone else was in the room until Mrs. Chivers said, "Here's Matty Brand, sir."

Without turning, Dr. Hobbes said, "Thank you, Mrs. Chivers. You may leave us."

I stayed where I was for what seemed a long time.

"Come closer to the fire, Matty," said Dr. Hobbes. "You must be cold."

I honestly didn't know if I was hot, or cold, or anything. I stepped up next to the armchair and said, "Please, sir, how is Miss Catherine?"

Dr. Hobbes lifted his right hand to his face and pinched the bridge of his nose between his thumb and index finger.

"She is sinking," he said wearily. "I took her to see a specialist in Norwich. He examined her thoroughly, but as I feared, he could offer no hope. I have brought her back to Tagram House so that she may die in familiar surroundings."

I was shocked.

"But, sir—" I said, then stopped myself, for

something about Dr. Hobbes's calm, level voice had reminded me of the hint of steel I'd glimpsed in him at our first meeting, and I held my tongue. I remembered the feeling I'd had that Dr. Hobbes was hiding something from me, and suddenly all kinds of new possibilities flashed into my head.

I'd assumed that Reuben was practising magic behind the master's back, but what if Reuben had been obeying Dr. Hobbes's instructions? Was it Catherine's guardian that Guido and Bella had tried to warn me about? Had Dr. Hobbes been play-acting the whole time? If so, then Tagram House was a more dangerous place than I'd thought, both for Catherine and for me. My new insights seemed to gape at me like a black mouth threatening to swallow me whole.

"Catherine's suffering will soon be over," said Dr. Hobbes.

It will be if I have anything to do with it! I thought, and said, "Can I see her, sir?" Dr. Hobbes stirred himself and looked at me, and once again I thought I saw the icy heart that lay deep within him.

"I am afraid she is far too weak, Matty," he said smoothly. "Besides, the sight of her might well distress you, and I'm sure that Catherine would not wish you to be distressed."

Was this the truth or was Dr. Hobbes deliberately keeping me from Catherine? What sinister reasons did he have for hiding her away?

"But I wouldn't—" I began to protest.

"That will be all, Matty," said Dr. Hobbes.

The matter was closed. He was the master, I was a servant in his house, and I was bound to obey.

The moment that I was out of Dr. Hobbes's presence, my shaky certainties collapsed into doubts. How could I possibly think ill of the master? He was an educated man who had been a professor at one of the greatest universities in the land. How could he have anything to do with ghosts and spells and dead children? And even if he had, what could I, a mere servant girl, do about it?

Puppets

19

I didn't eat supper so much as poke it into different places on my plate, and when it was time for bed I couldn't settle. It was as if a storm was gathering and bubbling inside me. Whenever I closed my eyes, I saw Catherine's grey face.

Mrs. Chivers had issued strict instructions that Catherine wasn't to be disturbed. The housekeeper announced that she would nurse the invalid and had shut herself in Catherine's room, locking both the door that led onto the landing, and the door that connected with my room.

It was maddening for me to be so close to Catherine and yet not able to go to her. I gave up sleep as a bad job, made a sort of chair of pillows on the floor and sat with my back resting against the door to Catherine's room. I wanted to be ready if I was needed suddenly in the night, so I didn't bother to get undressed and even kept my boots on.

To pass the time, I read a book that I'd borrowed from the schoolroom. It wasn't easy to read, what with the light of the candle making the words lurch this way and that over the page. The book I'd chosen, *Dark Fairies*, turned out to be heavy going: yet more tales of children dying. After a while I began to doze in dribs and drabs, and the people in the stories became people in my dreams.

Then the snick of a key in a lock roused me, and I opened my eyes. It was late. My candle had burned out, and the bedroom was dark. I heard movements in Catherine's room, whispers no louder than breaths being drawn, and I pressed my ear against the door. The whispers were too quiet for me to make out, but I heard enough to realize that Dr. Hobbes was paying Catherine a visit.

And then I sensed that I wasn't alone. I can't explain this properly because it's something older than words, but I sensed a presence near me, and I turned my head.

Guido stood at the foot of the bed, and he was staring at me. I wasn't afraid of him and I wasn't startled, because he was so still, and sad, and needing. He held both hands crossed over his chest.

"Guido?" I said.

He answered by lowering his hands and showing me the deep cuts on his wrists. The wounds gaped like mouths.

Guido spoke without moving his lips, in a voice that made no sound.

"*Il dottore,*" he said.

I shook my head to show that I didn't understand.

"*Per favore*," said Guido, gesturing to me. "*Per favore*."

"What d'you want?" I asked.

"*Caterina*," said Guido.

It was plain enough that he meant Catherine, and I stood up slowly.

"*Si, si!*" Guido said encouragingly. "*Per favore!*"

He beckoned me towards the door that led onto the landing, held up a hand to his ear and put his head to one side in a pantomime of listening.

I listened too, and heard a door closing and footsteps.

I opened my door a crack, peeped out and saw Dr. Hobbes walking away from Catherine's room.

"*Il dottore*," Guido said.

He waited for several minutes after Dr. Hobbes had gone, then took me down the servants' stairs to the back door.

I knew we were going to the shadow garden, the way it sometimes is in dreams when you know a thing without knowing how you know it.

A cold wind blew outside, driving clouds across the moon and stars. The air was fusty with the scent of decaying leaves.

Bella was waiting in the shadow garden. She greeted me with a bow, spread her arms and a puppet theatre appeared in front of her, with black curtains and tinplate footlights, and at once I was reminded that Guido and Bella's parents had been puppeteers. Strings hung down from Bella's fingers. The black curtains twitched, jerked and two puppets appeared, a boy and a girl, Guido and Bella in miniature. They were escaping from somewhere, running frantically through the night. They blundered into thick woods where there were no paths.

Guido went to stand beside his sister, and a third character came onto the stage, a figure that stalked the children without showing itself, apart from a pale gleam between the trunks of the trees, flitting like a moth from shadow to shadow.

Then the figure stood in front of the children, blocking their way. There was no mistaking who the puppet was meant to be, with its white sweeping hair and blue eyes. A little knife gleamed in the figure's right hand as it slashed at the children again and again. Their strings slackened, and they fell to the ground.

The puppet of Dr. Hobbes crouched to hold a silver bowl to the children's wounds, then raised the bowl to its lips – and the scene changed. Two graves had been dug in a garden, and the puppets of the children lay down in them.

The graves then vanished and a different child crossed the stage, a young girl with unruly black hair. Up above her, the puppet of Dr. Hobbes descended like a spider on its thread.

All my doubts about Dr. Hobbes evaporated. Guido and Bella's puppet show had made things clear to me at last. Dr. Hobbes was planning to do the same thing to Catherine as he had done to them – but why?

I blinked, and after the blink there was no theatre, no puppets, no Guido and Bella, just Reuben standing in the yew archway.

"I knew you'd come again," he said. "Couldn't keep away, could you?"

He was holding a sickle.

Blood Dance

20

A shaft of moonlight broke through the clouds and turned the blade of the sickle into a silver smile. Reuben stood as still as a gravestone, but I could feel his mind twisting and swirling.

I was afraid, but I wasn't going to give Reuben the satisfaction of knowing how afraid I was.

"Guido and Bella are buried in this garden, aren't they?" I said, and my voice sounded so steady and determined that it surprised me.

"Not far from where you're standing," said Reuben. "Master told me to put 'em there after he killed 'em. Winter it was. The ground was that hard I had to use a pickaxe. Later on, I planted the roses to cover 'em up."

"Why did Dr. Hobbes kill them?" I asked in a horrified whisper.

"For their blood," said Reuben. "It's all to do with blood, see. Blood dances round and round like them old stone circles. It's been dancing since the start of things. It dances in you all the days of your life, and when your blood gets tired, the dancing stops, and you go to your grave. That's the way of things – mostly."

It sounded to me as if Reuben was raving, but I wanted to keep him talking, in hope of catching him off his guard.

"What d'you mean, mostly?" I demanded.

Reuben laughed scornfully.

"The master's a tricky one!" he said. "He's read a lot of books that no one else has bothered with for years, and he reckons he's found a way out."

"A way out of what?" I said.

"The dance," said Reuben. "He takes young blood into him, and if he takes enough, he can cheat death for as long as he likes. He could live to be a thousand, and he won't look a day older than what he looks now. He'll be the most powerful man the world's ever seen, and he's sworn to share some of his power with them who's served him faithfully."

"Like you, I suppose," I said.

"Ah," Reuben said with a nod, "and Mrs. Chivers, and Mr. Vaughn, us who know enough to keep our mouths shut."

"He's going to murder Catherine," I said, shuddering at the thought.

"Some might call it murder," said Reuben, "others'd call it shifting power to where it's most needed. What does the life of a kiddy matter anyway? There's plenty more born every day. Everything would've gone as sweet as a nut if it hadn't been for you."

"Me?"

"It took me a while to find you out," said Reuben, "but then I thought it through. The moment you came here them Eye-talian kids' spirits got strong enough to be uppity, after I'd finally got 'em nice and quiet. They've been taking power from you, and I can't be doing with that. Upsets my magic, doesn't it?"

He sounded so calm, and sensible, yet totally insane.

I talked soothingly, gradually inching my way forwards to try and find a way of slipping past.

"You should let me go now, Reuben," I said. "You don't want Catherine dead. Help me to save her. I know you didn't mean anyone any harm. Dr. Hobbes tricked you with his clever words and mixed things up in your mind."

"Let you go?" snorted Reuben. "Course I can't let you go. You'll have to die along with the other brat, and the master'll take your blood as well as hers."

I was close to Reuben now.

"Stay back, witch!" he cried, raising the sickle.

And I kicked him in the pit of the stomach as hard as I could.

Reuben folded up like a clasp knife, his eyes bulging, his breathing making a sound like wet cotton tearing.

Someone stepped out of the shadows behind him and caught him a clout on the head that dropped him like a sack of coal being unloaded off the back of a cart.

To my amazement, it was Peg, with Mrs. Clark's second-best rolling pin in her hand. She stood over Reuben and prodded him with her toe.

"That should settle your nonsense, you old loon!" she muttered.

"Peg?" I said.

Peg glared at me.

"I know there's no love lost between us, Matty Brand, but we're the only two with any sense in this madhouse," she said. "I don't exactly know what's going on, but whatever it is, it ain't right and I've had a bellyful of it. I'm clearing off, now this minute, and I ain't coming back. What you do is up to you."

She half-turned.

"Wait!" I pleaded. "What about Catherine?"

"She ain't my concern," Peg said sulkily.

"If she doesn't leave this house tonight she'll die, and her death will be on your conscience," I said. "You have to get her away from Dr. Hobbes and Mrs. Chivers."

"And how am I going to do that?" Peg asked.

"Get Ma to help you," I said. "Let Ma distract Mrs. Chivers, then give Mrs. Chivers a taste of that rolling pin you're so handy with."

"And where'll I take Miss Catherine once I've got her?" said Peg.

I had a flash of inspiration.

"To Mrs. Clark's house in Derlingham," I said.

Suspicion darkened Peg's face.

"And what will you be doing while me and your ma are tootling about with Miss Catherine and Mrs. Chivers?" she said.

"I'll be having a word with Dr. Hobbes," I said.

I don't know what it was that convinced Peg to do

as I bid – perhaps the girl did have a conscience after all – but it worked a treat.

Most people describe rage as being hot and red, but that night my rage was cold and clear. I was angry for myself, for Catherine and especially for Guido and Bella. They had put their trust in Dr. Hobbes and he'd betrayed them, taken their lives because of some crackpot ideas that he'd found in a pile of musty books. Words like *ogre* and *monster* came into my mind, but Dr. Hobbes was worse than a monster. He was a man with a belief so strong that it blinded him to anything else. Love and hate, good and evil, right and wrong meant nothing to him any more.

I strode through the house as though I owned it and flung open the library door.

Dr. Hobbes was standing at the fireplace. He wheeled around and glared at me.

"Matty?" he said angrily. "What are you thinking of, barging in here without knocking?"

"I know what's buried in the rose garden," I declared boldly, "and I know about Catherine!"

Dr. Hobbes flinched for a second, then he relaxed, his manner almost casual.

"Do you now?" he said. "I must apologize for underestimating you, Matty. Reuben warned me about you, but I ignored him."

"You're not in your right mind, Dr. Hobbes," I said. "You can't conquer death, no one can."

Dr. Hobbes shrugged.

"Can they not, Matty?" he said. "Yet doctors strive to conquer death with medicines and surgery – should they give up their efforts because you say the conquest of death is impossible? Humans have dreamed of eternal life since they were first capable of thought. Many religions hold out the promise of immortality, take, for instance—"

"Don't try to bamboozle me!" I snapped. "Catherine's going away from here, and you'll never find her again because I'm going to tell the local constable everything."

Dr. Hobbes pursed his lips.

"I see," he said. "And I'm to simply stand by and let you, am I?" He laughed scornfully. "You're a courageous little thing, Matty, but you're no champion. I can snuff out your life like a candle flame and I shall take a great deal of pleasure in doing so."

He stepped towards me, his hands stretching out for my throat.

A rushing sound like a howling gale filled my ears, and I suddenly felt so weak that I could hardly stand. Time seemed to slow down to a crawl.

A mass of glowing orange lights was swarming around Dr. Hobbes. Then, like raindrops running together on a windowpane, the points of light slowly merged into two small figures. The last of my strength deserted me, and I sank to my knees as the shimmering forms of Guido and Bella appeared.

Dr. Hobbes stood stock-still. His eyes bulged and his lips twisted into a sneer.

"You hold no terrors for me!" he cried. "This world has done with you – begone!"

The children reached out to sweep their ghostly hands through Dr. Hobbes's body, and an orange glow ran up the arms of his jacket to his head and down to his feet. He rubbed his hands together to try and rid them of the glow.

Then, with a loud thump and a force that made me reel backwards, Dr. Hobbes burst into flames. He didn't have time to call out. One moment he was a man, the next he was a mass of seething fire. Flames spread across the library floor, like liquid spilling out of his burning body.

Despite my exhaustion I managed to stand up and stagger out through the opened door into the hall. Peg was coming down the stairs, and Ma, dressed in her night things, her hair tied up in rags. They were supporting Catherine between them. I rushed to the front door, heaved back the bolts, pulled the door open and ushered them through.

Just as I was about to step outside, I heard a terrible cry and Mrs. Chivers stumbled down the stairs holding one hand to the back of her head, shouting, "Master! Master!" She tottered into the library, and I never saw her again.

But I saw Guido and Bella, standing hand in hand in the library doorway, smiling at me as the fire roared and smoke billowed through Tagram House.

Eliza

21

Here's where my memory gets curdled and bitty, so I can't sort out what's real from what I was told after, or from what I've dreamed since.

I remember a door, and an angry voice, and the light of a storm lantern dazzling my eyes, so that must have been when we called at a farmhouse, and the farmer offered us a ride in his hay cart.

This part's clear: Catherine lying in the cart, covered with a moth-eaten old blanket, turning her head from side to side, muttering about the Dragon Man. I saw him then in my imagination, and I see him still, a creature with Dr. Hobbes's face, sweeping through the night sky on great black wings.

Then comes a humpty-backed bridge, gas lamps, buildings, more faces, more voices, darkness and dawn, a doctor, a policeman, a man who might have been a lawyer...

I can't be certain of any of it. I expect there's some fancy name for what was wrong with me, but the plain fact is that I was worn out after all I'd been through. My mind and spirit needed to take a holiday from the world, and so they did.

These are the facts.

Tagram House burned down. There was an inquest. I gave evidence, but I never told all that I knew, until now. I said that there was an accident in the library. The fire shifted in the grate and a burning ember was thrown onto one of the papers that were scattered over the floor, and the paper caught light. I know that it was wrong of me not to tell the truth when I was under oath, but I decided that a well-intentioned lie was better than a truth no one would believe.

The coroner recorded a verdict of accidental death on Dr. Hobbes, Mrs. Chivers and Mr. Vaughn, who was trapped upstairs by the fire. No trace of Reuben was ever found.

Since Dr. Hobbes had adopted Catherine as his ward, she inherited his estate, and once the lawyers had sold off the property, she was left with a tidy sum. Ma and I followed her to a new home. We had to, because for a long while Catherine and I could scarcely bear to be out of each other's sight. But time changes everything. Eventually Catherine *was* swept off her feet by the kind of handsome young gentleman I'd once wished for her, and not long afterwards I got married myself.

Guido and Bella never appeared to me again. Once Catherine was safe and their deaths had been avenged, their spirits could rest at last. They were at peace, but I wasn't, for I kept on going back to Tagram House in my dreams. Sometimes I'd wake up screaming after a dream of being trapped in Dr. Hobbes's blazing study, or shivering after a nightmare of being buried in the cold earth of the rose garden.

As I grew older, the dreams became less vivid and less frequent, but they still had the power to remind me of that terrible time. Then, six months ago, after my granddaughter Eliza was born, they returned as strong as ever.

Eliza is a pretty baby and good-natured, but goodness knows that when I look after her, she wears me thinner than any spirit ever did, and I've noticed something strange about her. Every so often when I lay her in her cot, she doesn't go to sleep straight away. She looks this way and that, gurgling and chuckling and kicking her heels, just as if someone was playing a game with her – except that no one's there.

This has set me wondering. Has the gift been passed on to Eliza, and is she already seeing spirits?

I can't say as yet. Things will be clearer when Eliza's older and can talk, but for the present there's nothing I can do but wait.

I've written down what happened at Tagram House and now I'm going to put away my writing somewhere safe, and there it'll stay until Eliza's old enough to read it for herself. Maybe she'll understand, maybe she won't, but I hope that what I've written will make the dreams leave me alone.

Time will tell.

Andrew Matthews has been writing for fun since he was seven, but was a teacher for twenty-three years before becoming a full-time author. He has written over sixty books for children and teenagers, including *Cat Song*, which was nominated for the Smarties Book Prize in 1994, and the critically acclaimed *Love Street*. He is a hugely versatile writer, and has retold many myths, legends and classic stories, as well as creating his own original picture books and novels.

Andrew lives in Reading with his wife and their cat.

If you have enjoyed

you might also like these other
spine-chilling reads...

Terry Deary
THE BOY WHO HAUNTED HiMSELF

There's no escape from the ghost in his mind.

When Peter Stone answers an advert promising to release the hidden power of the mind, he doesn't expect to find anything as squalid as the entrance to Dr. Black's office. And the mysterious doctor isn't quite what he seems either. But Peter is so determined to change his life that he ignores the warning signs...and then it's too late.

Powerless to escape an experiment that goes horribly wrong, Peter finds himself in a life-or-death struggle with an invader in his mind.

A truly creepy ghost story with a difference, from the author of the spectacularly successful *Horrible Histories*.

0 7460 6036 X

£4.99

Ann Evans

THE BEAST

How can you kill something that's already dead?

A beautiful, remote Scottish valley seems like the perfect holiday spot. But as soon as Amanda arrives with her family she senses that something is wrong.

No one will listen to her fears, even when she starts seeing mysterious shadows flitting across the mountainside, and strange scratches on her brother Grant's back.

Soon, Amanda and Grant are locked in a deadly battle with the beast that is haunting the Valley of Shadows...

A dark menace stalks the pages of this gripping and atmospheric thriller.

"Evocative and full of atmosphere...compelling and convincing." *The Guardian*

0 7460 6034 3

£4.99

Sandra Glover

DEMON'S ROCK

There's something evil out there...

Demon's Rock is feared by the locals. A place of
mystery and superstition, it is shrouded in tales of
dark forces and tragedy. Bug and Mona think this is
all superstitious nonsense. Until a strange boy turns
up on their doorstep one night, with an even stranger
tale to tell...

When Bug and Mona decide to investigate the
mysterious boy's story and his claims about the rock,
they are confronted by a truth much, much scarier
than any local legend.

A chilling, nightmare vision of the future is hidden
within the flames in this dark and compelling novel.

0 7460 6037 8

£4.99

Malcolm Rose

THE TORTURED WOOD

Who will be the next victim?

When Dillon's family moves into the tight-knit community of Bleakhill Top, Dillon soon discovers that the town is hiding a dark secret. His only refuge from the school bullies is in the wood that sccms to be at the very heart of the mystery. There Dillon finds some startling, eerie carvings in the rotting stumps and fallen trees. When he starts to investigate the mysterious sculptor, he finds himself in mortal danger.

The chilling atmosphere and tense, dramatic storyline of *The Tortured Wood* grab you by the throat on the first page and don't let go until the last.

> **"A gripping story... Good spooky stuff."**
> ***TES Teacher***

0 7460 6035 1

£4.99

Paul Stewart

THE CURSE OF MAGORiA

Will anyone escape the deadly dance of time?

According to local legend, Magoria was a powerful sorcerer intent on harnessing time itself. But his experiments went disastrously wrong, and he unlocked a dangerous curse that could strike the mountain village of Oberdorf at any time.

When Ryan arrives there on holiday he has no idea that his visit might have deadly consequences...that he might unleash the Curse of Magoria.

A breathtaking tale of dark magic, adventure and revenge from the co-author of the hugely successful series *The Edge Chronicles*.

"Mysterious forces are abroad in this nail-biting tale." *Carousel*

0 7460 6232 X

£4.99